A Town Called Limbo

Loner Buck Dulane was not looking for trouble when a lonesome trail brought him to the river town. But a strange young man, a ruthless band of raiders from Old Mexico and an ever deepening murder mystery involving the entire town changed all that.

Could one man save those who desperately needed him? And would anybody survive a town called Limbo?

A Town Called Limbo

Dempsey Clay

A Black Horse Western

ROBERT HALE · LONDON

© Dempsey Clay 2006
First published in Great Britain 2006

ISBN-10: 0-7090-8180-4
ISBN-13: 978-0-7090-8180-7

Robert Hale Limited
Clerkenwell House
Clerkenwell Green
London EC1R 0HT

Typeset by
Derek Doyle & Associates, Shaw Heath
Printed and bound in Great Britain by
Antony Rowe Limited, Wiltshire

CHAPTER 1

BORDER RIDER

Buck Dulane rode down out of the Sunstreak Hills by moonlight and crossed the line by the stone section-marker which was about all that remained of the old Lazy S ranch of other days.

The town came into sight, a glowing patch of light two miles distant across the flatlands with the glinting ribbon of Diablo Creek visible beyond, where it wound and coiled towards its rendezvous with the Majestic River.

The lone rider travelled easily with his free right hand resting on his hip and handy to the butt of the .45 riding his hip. He smoked a cheroot and there was relaxation and ease in the way he sat his saddle, yet alertness glimmered in the dark eyes. In this kind of country a man could never afford totally to relax anyplace, not even when a combination of deep moonshadows, wide-open vistas and an innocent-seeming stretch of trail stretching ahead might lull him into doing so.

He was travelling downslope as he flicked away the cigar butt, then suddenly stiffened in the saddle as another sound reached up to him from the timbered slope off to his right and some distance below.

Just the way he whipped the .45 from leather and cocked it in the same motion would have been a warning to anyone watching that this man was no stranger to danger – if indeed it was danger he was scenting now.

Seemed like it could be.

As he halted the bay between the twin joshua trees on the flank of the shale slope, the sounds of muffled hoofbeats drifting down from someplace higher came clearer. Just the one set, now louder, then fainter, carrying unevenly to his ears on the faintest whisper of a breeze.

Not border patrollers; they never ventured this far out here where heat-blasted Sonora and desert-raddled Arizona fused together somewhere in the great vastness between Yuma and Nogales.

Bandits? Not likely. Nothing to steal here worth braving the heat and desolation for. An Arizonan lawman hunting some border-jumping hellion, maybe? He was skeptical about that even though it might rate as a long-shot possibility. For there were any number of the wanted breed about the border-lands this time of the year, and Buck Dulane was one of them. The horse trembled nervously. He soothed it with a fingertip touch and continued to hold it still. Against the clouds limned by starlight he likened the

6

joshua trees to Indian ceremonial dancers raising arms to the sun gods.

Or maybe praying for him?

Dulane tugged his hatbrim low and with slitted eyes probed the uncertainty of the night. Rangy and tough, gun-quick and aggressive, especially when cornered, he was leaving a mess of trouble in back of him down south but had no good reason to believe this stretch of borderland should hold any particular risks for him. The troubles he'd encountered, created, triumphed over or had run from were all far behind now with no significant loose ends left over, so far as he knew. He was as free and easy of conscience as any hustling *Americano* loner might be on heading home at the end of a winter of danger, drifting, sharp deals and the occasional bloody violence which was all part of life in sunny Mexico.

So why should he feel uneasy now simply because there was a horseman up there someplace where he hadn't expected there to be anything other than the occasional gopher, cougar or shriek-owl?

Experience was the reason, of course. Never assume you were safe anyplace; never take a fool chance when you don't have to.

He was prepared to wait as long as it took to find out who that unseen horseman could be before giving the bay its head again.

The nightwind raised a thin dust cloud of alkali in the draws and branch canyons which turned into silver tendrils in the starlight. The bay blew a nervous breath and in that instant the sound of that other horse abruptly ceased. Suddenly Dulane was no

7

longer merely watchful. In the space of a heartbeat he was totally alert with every nerve screwed up tight as he felt the very air come alive with the brassy taste of menace.

Times like this Buck Dulane had the patience of a hunter. With his Colt .45 at shoulder height and pointed skywards with a finger curled around the trigger, he sat his saddle calmly, ready either to open up or use his spurs, depending on what he might see up there on that higher slope, which at the moment was nothing more defined than a long gray hump in the feeble light.

Something whistled high overhead above the wind-lifted dust, followed by the sharp thud and rattle of something striking rocks in back of him before clattering away into silence.

Dulane spat out the match he was chewing and licked dry lips. An unseen hand had tossed something – most likely a pebble – which had landed behind him, possibly to divert his attention from the slope.

The way he figured it, someone could either see him or had at least heard his horse. He figured they likely wanted either to scare him on his way or trick him into revealing himself so they might get to cut him down.

He'd taken the right precaution in setting himself up between the joshuas. Now, as he hunkered lower over the horse's neck, eyes cut to a single steely gleam, he doubted he could be seen, but had no doubts that someone was close. The roar of the rifle came shockingly loud.

Instantly Dulane slipped to ground and whipped his Winchester from its scabbard before darting for the cover of the closest joshua tree.

'Stand, you jackass, stand!' he hissed, and the trembling bay obediently stood its ground.

He knew where the rifleman was now.

The flash had erupted from the upper crest of the slope close by a canting yellow boulder. His first impulse was to cut loose and splatter the boulder with some fast fire. He didn't succumb to the temptation and moments later was glad of it.

'We are Truenos!' the powerful American voice shouted. 'Show yourself and be identified!'

Truenos!

That was no name to trifle with here or anyplace else in the Southwest. Both up here and across the border, where he'd plied his gun-trade that winter, the rebel Fidel Trueno had a chilling reputation as a ruthless Mexican landowner-cum-*bandido*, leading a band of revolutionary and cold-blooded killers feared throughout the Palo Pinto region. He'd rarely heard of 'Truenos' being sighted this far north this time of year.

He was on the verge of replying to establish his 'innocent' credentials when he heard the sudden clatter of another rider moving further to the west along the crest.

That meant there were two of them at least and they were trying to circle him! Dulane's jaws locked tight.

Nothing in his background had given him reason to take fool chances. From Michigan he'd gone off to

Kansas during the war where he'd served his apprenticeship as a guerrilla fighter with the Walker brigade in that border state, and from there had taken up gunfighting in the post-war years before finding his way down to Mexico. For two years he'd hired out to fight rustlers, guerrilla bands and occasionally the corrupt border armies of Old Mexico. It was the sort of experience to make any man expert at staying alive.

He could fight with the fury of a cornered dog-wolf when put to it, but was always wary of a situation where there was no way of accurately calculating the odds. Only a fool rushed in to brace danger blind.

If there were two riders up there along that slope, in his thinking that meant there could just as easily be ten. Experience had taught him the Truenos rarely did things by halves.

He took his time reaching a decision then acted upon it real fast.

He hit saddle in a flying jump and the jittery bay covered fifteen feet in its first explosive leap. The horse hit ground running as both rifle and sixgun erupted like a cannonade behind, to lend wings to flying hoofs. Dulane took the streaking horse down a steep-sided gully-wash at breakneck speed, then rounded a crumbling stone buttress to find a canyon opening before him. He hesitated only momentarily; the open canyon offered easy running but little cover. But as speed was plainly called for here, he heeled the bay onwards to go storming out across the hard-packed floor, all stops out and angling north.

He was feeling safer by the minute after putting

the canyon well in back of him without attracting any further gunfire. He heaved a sigh of relief as he went clattering across a cactus-dotted ridge to go hammering down into a rapidly changing stretch of terrain.

Here was a mazelike tangle of hogbacks and gulches, empty as a politician's promise in some stretches, then choked up with brush and rocks in others, where he was forced to cut around and negotiate, slowing almost at the walk. But the high shoulders of the gulch provided excellent cover and he might have felt totally safe but for that give-away pall of hoof-lifted dust.

But no man with a single wheel in his thinkbox was going to allow a detail like that slow him down while he was making good time.

Speed was again required now and he was utilizing it to the full when he suddenly emerged from a ravine to find himself on a long and open slope where he instantly sighted a pair of horsemen cutting down towards him from a cedar-studded black bluff off to his right.

He cursed viciously when he heard them shout again before gunflame flared to send him bolting recklessly towards a jagged-mouthed ravine, with his neck hair lifting in alarm. A glance over his shoulder caught a glimpse of black sombreros and his heart skipped a beat.

These bastards were almost certainly who they claimed to be, he figured now. Those high-domed black sombreros were almost like a badge for the Truenos. He reckoned that by now they'd figured him an enemy and were plainly intent on running

11

him down. That warned him it was high time to get serious. Dead serious.

He started off by taking his chasers for a ride.

Riding hands and heels he went storming through another scrubby patch of mesquite before picking up a faint trace of trail stretching across a quarter mile of upslope. This led to a section where huge boulders tumbling down from higher up forced the trail to wind its way circuitously between them.

He continued to drive the bay with hands and heels to maintain a headlong gallop, his pursuers not appearing through the mesquite behind until the first boulders were already closing around him.

Instantly he reined the horse to a dust-billowing halt and was out of the saddle, his fist clutching cheekstrap and rifle as dust of their own making engulfed both man and mount.

A gun crashed. Somewhere above he could hear the deep grunting of the horses coming downhill towards him at a reckless gallop.

The racing riders were less than fifty yards distant when Dulane came ghosting out of his concealing dust-fog in a low crouch with the rifle clapped to his shoulder.

He cut loose.

Instantly the lead horse went down on its nose, the rider propelled high in limb-waving flight that ended with the sickening crunch of a body striking rocky ground. The man bounced high again, eyes bulging and a broken arm dangling uselessly. An hysterical scream ripped from his throat when the Winchester bellowed again with fierce authority and a whistling

.32 ripped a hole through his chest.

Dulane's expression didn't alter as he watched the body smack ground and roll like something that had never known life.

Passionless, he was instantly focused on the second horseman.

The man was veering wildly away . . . and Dulane's lips curled in contempt. He was a fool! He'd left it far too late to run now. Should have kept on coming at him with both guns blazing. That's what Buck Dulane would have done in his boots. Luckily he wasn't.

The Winchester bucked in his hands and gunflame lanced across a hundred yards of open space.

It was only chance that saw the horse toss its head at that vital last moment. Dulane heard the ugly thud of his bullet smacking bone. Horse bone. The animal crashed and somersaulted in full stride and the rider was entangled in leather straps beneath its rolling bulk for long seconds before he could kick clear of the stirrups. Tumbling end over end in a wild tangle of limbs and legs, man and horse churned downhill past his crouching figure and Dulane had the man's head fixed in his gunsights when curiosity stayed his hand.

He already knew they wanted to kill him; suddenly he wanted to know why. He darted forward as the half-dazed gunman eventually became disentangled, struggled to stop rolling and got himself into a shooting position. 'Reach, you dry-gulching son of a bitch!' roared Dulane.

13

The man in black reeled back against his dead claybank, dashing at his eyes and fumbling for the belt gun that wasn't there any more. Buck Dulane's finger was itchy on the trigger but somehow he held his fire. Moving in closer, he motioned the man to rise. He was big and ugly with hands the size of dinner-plates, and the blood seeping from cuts and scrapes didn't improve his appearance any. He might be dazed and hurting but that didn't dim the murderous look in his eyes.

He struggled to claw out his sixgun. Dulane realized that he was American, which only fanned his fury. Shouting to confuse the man further, he rushed in on him with pantherlike speed and reversed the Winchester more quickly than the eye could follow to smash the butt to the side of the head with brutal impact. The man's big boots actually left the ground before he landed on his back in deep dust and lay motionless like a man who might never move again.

'You can sleep later, scum,' Dulane growled and jabbed the rifle muzzle into the throat.

Next moment he found himself in trouble.

Displaying amazing resilience his catch snapped his eyes open, seized the Winchester barrel and jerked violently.

Dulane might have pulled trigger and finished it then and there. But he didn't. Instead he drove a vicious knee to the groin and the bigger man howled, staggered yet still didn't go down. But he did buckle and clutch at his groin as he gasped out an accusing: 'Stinkin' mercenary son of a bitch!'

Then he counter-attacked.

14

He moved blindingly fast and Dulane barely managed to sway out of reach as the huge bulk brushed him by.

Ducking low under clawing hands, he drove in hard with his shoulder into his attacker's rib box, drawing a sucked-in gasp of pure agony and a flying elbow by way of retaliation.

The elbow did not miss.

Downed and dazed in a heartbeat, Dulane fuzzily realized that his face was bare inches from the ground while his head buzzed like a swarm of angry bees. He'd had the bastard at his mercy, yet suddenly their positions were reversed and he was now in deep trouble!

The hell he was!

He rolled violently as a spurred boot came slamming into the earth where he'd been lying. His adversary readied to let loose another kick. Dulane seized the sweeping foot and threw all the power of wide shoulders and leathery arms into giving it a truly vicious twist.

The big man screamed and crashed to ground, clutching a dislocated knee. Dulane made it to his feet, eyes blazing. One good kick deserved another, he always insisted. His boot crashed home against short ribs and bones cracked audibly. He was angling for a potentially fatal kick to the temple when, above his attacker's groans of agony, he heard yet again the drumming of hoofbeats.

Some of the rage began to drain from Dulane's features as he backed away from the agonized giant. The scene before him comprised one dead horse off to his right, a crippled mount limping away to the left and a second, hatchet-faced man sprawled in the careless attitude of violent death fifty feet away.

He shook his head.

He'd figured he'd said goodbye to all this on quitting Santa Rita. Indeed, the main reason he'd elected to quit after half a year of big money and high danger down South had been a sudden craving for change backed up by a sharpened hunger for the comparative peace and quiet of his homeland.

It seemed to him now, mired yet again in a scene of violence and death, that Old Mexico – turbulent, bewitching, hot-blooded Mexico – was making one desperate last attempt to claim him before he could complete what he'd sworn would be his final border crossing.

He shook his head.

He wouldn't let that happen.

Without another glance at the crippled survivor in the tall grass he went jogging back to the rocks, swung astride his horse, and dug.

Nobody gave chase either then or later.

He rode on through the remainder of the night without encountering anything more dangerous than the occasional butterfly-sized Mexican mosquito. Daylight found him travelling at an easy walk across the sifting sands and basalt rock-rubble of Arizona.

Limbo did not care for strangers.

This fact of life was becoming clear to the new arrival from the south by mid-afternoon that day when half the town closed down for siesta while the other half patronized the single saloon.

These social patterns reflected Limbo's history and background. Twenty years earlier the town had been mostly Mexican even though located north of the border.

Then the first flood of pale-skinned and blue-eyed migrants arrived to introduce American power, money and arrogance into one of the loneliest, most desolate outposts in the sprawling Southwest for the first time.

The Spanish influence still showed strong in the adobes, the fiestas and the squat stone church which still attracted a reasonable congregation at Sunday mass. They contrasted sharply with false-fronts, shabby stores, a honkytonk and a couple of clapboard saloons and the weary sprawl of the Wells Fargo Overland Mail depot.

This isolated hodge-podge combination of two cultures seemed wisely named; Limbo was the halfway station between Heaven and Hell in the Bible and at times Limbo on the Majestic River might appear halfway between dead and alive. The closest town was sixty miles north of the border and it was treble that distance to the nearest decent hotel, law office, bank or bordello.

You could shrivel up and die in a place like this. Some did. But most survived and a few even thrived, despite isolation, furnace heat and their just once-weekly contact with the outside world through the stage line.

Despite its dry and harsh surroundings here in its

remote seclusion along the banks of the big river, the town itself was curiously and eerily shaded by huge protective pecan trees, all gnarled and gray with long tatters of dead bark that hung like ragged ribbons and offered contrast to the dense, light-green foliage of heavy cedars.

It was this encirclement of secretive trees which gave an atmosphere of enclosure to a place that seemed at most times almost to be cut off from the reality of the outside world. This atmosphere was accentuated by the presence of people with strange names and odd habits who created the impression that some travellers during the western expansion had stopped by here, found it to their liking, stayed and settled while progress swept on by.

There was a battered old church with a tilting steeple where some people prayed to God, while next door but two was the strangely scented dwelling of a young-old woman who could cast spells and at times see into the future.

Wolves howled here at night and more than once hungry mountain lions had come dangerously near before being driven away by citizens with guns.

It was the vain perception of the members of the Pioneer Club that they thrived best of all, and apart from a few jealousy-motivated critics principally of the gambling-drinking persuasion of which Limbo had more than its fair share, most in town were inclined to agree.

Certainly the Pioneers set whatever tone was to be found here, and numbering as it did amongst its members such 'luminaries' as a retired government official, the proprietress of the Cobweb Palace saloon, a former peace officer from Tucson and the Wells Fargo agent, this might well have been a some-what higher tone than a place like this warranted.

But overwhelmingly Limbo, with its low-running river and backdrop of brooding hills was a hardcase community where good times were hard to come by and people were at liberty to just go to hell any which way they pleased without too many do-gooders, Samaritans or concerned representatives of church or state bothering greatly whether you lived or died, providing you didn't bother anyone too much or frighten the horses while you were about it.

Somehow the Club had survived here, and stub-bornly if infrequently set time aside to come together and indulge in their lofty preferences for gossip, wine-tastings, and literary discussions mixed liberally with their often venomous attacks upon local identi-ties, outrages, superstitions and tatty events.

Today was such a day and the 'extraneous busi-ness' raised by Jean Kelly was the arrival of the lone rider from the south, visible at that very moment from their north windows, directly across the street lounging upon the gallery of the single-floor hotel, legs outstretched and hat tilted forward onto his nose beneath a haze of tobacco smoke.

'His name is Dulane – or so he says,' supplied this former, fading dance-hall rose who now ran the only decent saloon in town. 'And says that his business is guns and horses – which could mean anything. We have seen his kind before often enough, and mostly we can't wait to see the back of them. But for some

19

reason this one appears to have a glimmer of quality or character about him, don't you think? Or am I alone in this opinion?'

She was met with curious looks.

The only female member and the driving force behind this tiny bastion of taste and refinement in a basically primitive society, Jean Kelly rarely displayed interest in mundane matters such as new arrivals, was much more suited to displaying knowledge and spouting opinions on such matters as the latest book of French poetry, high fashion, or political reports from Washington – when not drawing beers and having drunks thrown out of her place, that was.

Henri the Painter and Mr Branson were moved to tilt forward in badly worn chairs to peer through glazed windows in order to study the recent arrival, yet both appeared unmoved and unstimulated as they leaned back and picked up their wine-glasses again.

'Border-jumper,' insisted Henri. He enumerated on his long and slender fingers. 'Criminal record in the United States, known to Mexican authorities, unmarried, no specific trade or profession, immoral, alcoholic and congenitally violent and, at best, only an outside chance to reach thirty.' He smiled at his own cleverness. 'That breed is just a dime a dozen, Miss Jean. Surely you agree, Mr Branson?'

Despite their snobbery and lofty aspirations there was an underlying vulnerability and a genuine need for the strength of unity which the Clubbers found amongst their fellow members of the Pioneers, with the exception of Ethan Branson, the retired official from further east, that was. Only Branson, whose military bearing, silver hair and craggy visage stamped him as being genuinely superior, might have fitted easily and naturally into the most exclusive and influential clubs and societies of places like Phoenix, San Francisco or Santa Fe. This man was a large fish in a small pond with a surprisingly wide knowledge of and interest in matters legal, who regarded himself as an expert on the exotic mix of characters ranging from the very good down to the very bad who might filter their way through to Limbo in the course of any bordertown year. Nobody really understood what had driven a man of Branson's obvious education and experience to settle in a town like theirs.

'Trouble with a capital T,' was Branson's affirming opinion, although it was plain to see that he felt the subject of the newcomer didn't really warrant serious attention. 'And now perhaps we can move on to—'

'Yet I still wonder why it is that I feel this man might be something rather better than our usual brand of footloose loser?' Jean Kelly persisted contrarily, her manner preoccupied now as she gazed from the window again.

Sharp glances were exchanged behind the woman's back at this, for it was known here in the Club, just as it was out on the harsh streets of this frame-and-adobe backwater, that although seemingly armoured against the advances of all would-be suitors from Mr Branson himself down to town drunk Irish O'Neil, the still attractive Miss Jean, fading by the year in this forgotten gloom town, was just a sad and secretly yearning romantic at heart.

Was it possible, they wondered, that in this stranger Miss Jean might be seeing her last chance to fulfil her secret dreams of romance?

Nobody knew anything about the impressive newcomer but they seriously doubted he would prove any different from the one before him and the one before that. It was an accepted belief of borderland life that virtually anyone and everyone who came to Limbo had to be somehow crippled, deprived or twisted to want to stay on. Even the august members of the Pioneer's Club understood this about themselves even if they would never concede it in so many words.

Limbo was for losers; none could argue with that.

And should that wide-shouldered stranger in the yellow hat and roper's gloves stay on longer than a few days, in their cynical eyes that would would brand him as a loser also.

Meantime, lazily unaware of this sharp scrutiny as he loafed back loose-limbed and relaxed, Buck Dulane sank even deeper into his canvas-backed rocking-chair and scratched his belly in a lazy, self-contented way.

He was feeling good despite the fact that the violent Mexico he'd figured he was leaving far behind had made one last perverse effort to reach out and claw him back to help fill that bottomless grave into which so many of his high-riding compatriots had vanished over the years.

He grinned lazily.

Old Mexico's last-ditch attempt to bring him down right on the border had failed and Dulane was feeling secure, chipper and self-satisfied as he soaked up Arizona sun and digested Arizona vittles. And wondered whether, with just a little bit of luck, he might get to round it all out with some 'lucky' Arizonan woman.

He felt like a man who'd slipped the undoubtedly just punishment for his many sins, and thanked seedy Limbo for it. He would be in no hurry to quit this lost and forgotten old adobe town, he mused. He had the good feeling that a lazy month spent here reacquainting himself with his own people and customs might erase the bad memories and set him up as good as new again. And he barely spared a thought now for the curious and violent events that had overtaken him back in the border hills. He was living the here and now, and it was good.

CHAPTER 2

When he walked into the Cobweb Palace that night around seven the newcomer to town was looking refreshed and feeling great. Nothing like a long, steaming tub, rub-down with big fleecy towels, shave, trim and a generous slathering of lavender-water to set a man up before climbing into freshly laundered rig, torching a fresh cigarette and swaggering out to hit the town.

Of course, the phrase 'hitting the town' didn't quite have the same ring to it as it did in places such as Juárez, Prescott or Tombstone, where there might be a dozen saloons-cum-whorehouses-cum-gambling-halls to explore, droves of pretty women to get into serious trouble over, any number of young blades eager for friendship, a fight or even a duel to the death – if the whiskey was strong enough and the moon was in the right quarter to strip away inhibitions and encourage wonderful violence.

High life in Limbo meant either the Cobweb Palace saloon or the Gila Hotel. After that, forget it. But for a man who felt he'd seen rather too much of Mexican

life, both high and lowdown in Diaz City, everything
that met his eye here tonight appeared strange, almost
eerie, yet paradoxically new and non-threatening, as
he sauntered to the bar. Just the way he liked it.

As luck would have it, it was the bartender's supper
hour and the proprietress herself was serving.

Dulane flashed his best smile and threw a lean leg
over a high stool, flashing his fat roll just to make
sure she knew he could pay. 'Double rye and beer
chaser, beautiful. Oh yeah . . . and a smile.'

Miss Jean Kelly's disciplined features remained
blank as she filled the order. 'My name is Miss Kelly,
Mr Dulane. That will be two bits, thank you.'

He paid cheerfully. 'How come you know my
name, Miss Kelly?' He winked. 'That how it is with
everyone who drifts into your town, or am I something special?'

'I'm sorry to tell you I simply make it my business
to know everyone who comes and goes.'

'Well, for a minute there you had me going. Care
to join me for one or two, Miss er. . . ?'

'Kelly.'

'I'm trying to guess your first name. You know, I
see you as a Loren. Or maybe a Helen. Yeah, Helen
fits you just fine, ladylike, pretty and high-class.' He
finished this sally off with the killer smile but was
wasting his energies.

'You'll have to excuse me,' he was told as she
moved away. 'Yes, what will you have, Eli?'

In the secret part of her that dreamed of a life far
different from this, Miss Jean might see a strange
face and feel some faint tug of the heartstrings as she

perhaps had ten years earlier when she was a whole lifetime younger. But the years were slowly stealing away her radiance while compensating with strength and wisdom. She could still dream but no longer either hoped or believed. This stranger was surely handsome and charming, but obviously nothing more. She knew that underneath the veneer he would eventually prove to be just as selfish and self-centered as every other Clint, Darcy or Jack who'd shouldered through her batwings over the years. Plainly he had nothing for her.

Dulane had no notion what she was thinking and it wouldn't have changed a thing if he had. He fed the fish lines and they were free either to bite or not. It never went deeper than that with Buck Dulane. All he needed to set him up was to get this double down, cleanse the tongue with a following cooling ale – and then he would be ready for anything or anybody the Limbo night had to offer.

A hand fell on his shoulder, causing him to grab his gun handle and whirl before remembering where he was. And that was – back in a safe Arizonan saloon in a strange, strange town and one hell of a long way from Diaz City. A drunk stood weaving before him, black curls tumbled across a broad forehead.

'Got the price of a cup of coffee, stranger?'

'Mr O'Neil!' Miss Jean's voice sounded sharply. 'I've warned you about cadging on my premises, haven't I? Kindly leave Mr Dulane be.'

'Dulane?' the drunk said wonderingly. 'Dulane and O'Neil! Faith but it must be Old Ireland week. Just one little drink perhaps and—'

26

'Sorry.'

Dulane didn't give handouts. Didn't believe in them. He'd come up harder than any ten men he knew, yet he had never cadged a dime. Cheated on occasion, stolen from time to time, yes. But never panhandled. Rules you lived by. Like never sitting with your back to a saloon door. Or falling in love with a madam of the bordello.

Irish O'Neil shook his sorry head. He turned to look pleadingly at the drinkers of the Club. But it was as if his eye had ptomaine poisoning; nobody wanted to catch it.

By and large Limbo was a remote and inbred melting-pot of a town. But even here they had their standards and it was generally agreed that this red-nosed rum-dum and back-alley dosser was right down at the bottom of just about everybody's social list.

There was another reason apart from his drinking-habits that ensured the drunk's lowly status, which Dulane was unaware of as yet, but wouldn't be for long

'Here,' Miss Jean said, plonking a brimming glass down on the bartop. 'Drink it and leave, Mr O'Neil.'

It was sarsaparilla. Irish O'Neil suddenly resembled the leading character in a Greek tragedy who has just been informed that barbarians have burned his crops, raped his wife and eaten his favorite dog. 'Sars!' he groaned. But revulsion didn't stop him from grabbing up the glass and gulping down the contents as though in practice for the real thing, if the real thing should ever come his way again.

Dulane clapped the man amiably on the shoulder,

then quit the bar to join the blackjack players. He invested and won, then won again. The croupier was young and pretty, which he liked, wore a low-cut dress and a big smile, which he really liked.

'Fancy yourself . . . as a player, mister?'

'I've got ten dollars here to say I can beat the bank, honey.' He stepped closer to the table and felt his leg brush something that moved. He looked down. Nothing. Curiously he lifted the corner of the table-sheet and found himself staring into the grubby face of a child of around three or maybe four, clutching a toy rifle. 'What the hell. . . ?'

'Oh . . . Boy Johnny!' chided the girl. 'You're supposed to stay out of sight. You know Miss Jean doesn't allow children in here.' She pulled a wry face at Dulane. 'He really shouldn't be in here, but I can't help feeling he's better off here than on the streets.'

Dulane stared at the kid. He didn't have much to do with children but this one seemed to have some special spark about him, he mused. 'Here you go, kid.' Perfunctorily, he produced a coin and flipped it to the boy. It was a shiny double-eagle, tangible evidence that any man handy with a Colt .45 could make good money down in Mexico these days, providing he wasn't too scared of dying young.

'Better get out of here like the lady says, kid. Go buy yourself some chow.'

'Or a gun?' The child beamed, testing the coin with his teeth. 'Ellie, is this enough to buy a real gun?'

The girl played out a hand and announced a five-minute break. She boxed the cards, looked around,

28

then drew the boy out from under, deliberately blocking him off from sight of the bar with her body. Dulane clicked his chips and, standing casually with one hip outthrust, put on a frown.

'What do you want with a gun, kid?' he demanded sternly. 'Don't you have enough troubles already? Guns are trouble. Even a tad like you ought to know that.' And knew how hypocritical that must sound with him sporting twin Colts plus a sneak .22 shoved up his sleeve.

'Hear what the man says, Johnny?' said the girl. 'Anyway, that's not nearly enough money for a gun. And even if it was, your uncle wouldn't let you have one.'

'He's got kin?' asked Dulane.

Ellie threw him a look then inclined her head toward the bar. 'In a manner of speaking,' she said.

Following her eyeline Dulane saw Irish O'Neil still savoring his sarsaparilla, making it last in the slender hope some Samaritan might wander along and spice it up with five fingers of black rum. 'You mean. . . ?'

'Yes. That's Boy Johnny's uncle, isn't it, honey?' she affirmed, ruffling the kid's hair. He was fair-haired and blue-eyed with a gravity of manner that was curiously engaging. Ellie brushed his hair back out of his eyes and pinched his snub nose. 'Had anything to eat tonight?'

'Can you eat a lion, Ellie?' he replied.

'Kids!' Dulane snorted. 'First guns, now lions. Aren't there any normal kids about anymore?'

The girl sat and swung the child on to her lap, and only now did Dulane belatedly notice pert breasts and finely sculpted features. Mother and Child, he thought. Only thing wrong with the picture was that girls like Ellie didn't have kids, and kids like this didn't need blackjack dealers for mommies. 'We're not talking about any old lion, are we, Johnny?' She smiled understandingly.

The kid shook his head solemnly as he gazed up at the man.

'*La Sombra*,' he said portentously.

'The shadow?' Dulane said, perplexed.

'You've not heard of that critter yet?' the girl asked. She gestured. 'Everyone claims there's been a big cat taking cattle in the foothills recently, and it's supposed to have killed two men on the Rafter K. Hunters claim it came up from Mexico.' Her eyes twinkled at him. 'Most trouble comes from Mexico, seems to me.'

'Hmm,' was Dulane's enigmatic response. Suddenly he was growing less interested in children and pumas and more so in pretty blackjack dealers again . . . and the night seemed to stretch enticingly ahead. 'Ellie? That your name? Why don't you and I go looking for real trouble?'

'Oh-oh,' warned the girl. 'I think trouble's already coming.'

O'Neil had just sighted his kid. He came weaving through the crowd, his face blotched and angry. 'What'd I tell you, brat?' he shouted, fumbling for his belt. 'A hundred times I've warned you – keep out of the saloon. You want to give your uncle a bad name? All right, Ellie, give him over. It's time I taught him a lesson he won't forget in a hurry.'

'Please, Irish, don't punish him,' she urged. 'He's got to be somewhere.'

'Not in here,' the man replied, dragging the boy from her lap with a long bony hand. 'Not where he'll make me look bad, which is just what he wants to do, so I'm thinkin'. Well, he won't be doin' it again in a hurry. Bend over, you little devil! Bend, I say!'

Dulane had already started off, not wishing to get involved. Limbo for him represented peace and quiet, some good lazy drinking and maybe a little tender lovemaking to ease away the sixgun tensions of the South. He felt like a man who'd had himself a bellyful of trouble for now. His long-term goal here was to not create one single ripple of trouble or excitement while relaxing and recovering in this sleepy backwater.

Yet when he saw a bony hand raise a doubled belt-strap high, he suddenly found himself moving back to the blackjack table. Real fast.

His hand wrapped around O'Neil's wrist and his fingers dug into flesh and bone with such force that the man cried out in agony and dropped to his knees to the floor. Boy Johnny straightened and stared up at him before the girl whisked him up in her arms to vanish in back. Onlookers gaped. Dulane just smiled to show it was 'all good fun', but the drunk's agonized look and staring eyes belied this.

It seemed suddenly to go quiet in the Cobweb Palace.

'Hey, what's all the fuss, folks?' Dulane grinned, releasing his grip and helping the man to his feet. He brushed dust off Irish O'Neil's ragged coat then produced a five-spot. 'Bit of horseplay never hurt anyone, eh, Irish? Go get yourself a real drink – and the top of the evening to you, boyo.' Then hissed under his breath, 'And leave the kid alone . . . next time I'll snap your arm off and make you eat it – dung-eater!'

This was more like the Buck Dulane known, liked and occasionally feared and hated in places far from Limbo where his contrasting lazy charm and sudden violences seemed to attract both friends and enemies with equal ease.

Hurting and humiliated, Irish O'Neil scuttled off for the bar and the murmur of conversations gradually rose again. The piano started up afresh and Dulane stood trying to see just how many drinkers he could attract and impress with his 'Honest, it was just a bit of horseplay' expression of quizzical affability.

Jean Kelly's eyes followed him as he threaded through the customers looking for pretty Ellie. Unconsciously the most attractive and unavailable woman in Limbo licked her lips with a small pointed tongue tip.

The following three days saw Dulane relax while maintaining a watchful eye upon the south.

The spot he'd found best-suited to this harmless-seeming activity was atop the water-tower which loomed in red-rust splendor above the general store and the chop-house on Gibson Street off Chisum. There was a windmill that pumped water from the river into the tank from which the townsfolk in turn drew their supplies. The sentry-box-sized little room of plank and tin erected atop the tank for the use of the druggist when he clambered up here to test the water purity once a week, was a comfortable place to sit and smoke and fiddle with his collapsible Army telescope, whose all-seeing prisms had saved the Dulane neck more than once down South.

Nothing showed from that direction during that time but for a ragged Mexican family forsaking the rigors of life in Baja California for the promised land of the USA, a paint salesman who must surely go bust in largely unpainted Limbo, and a long-haired circus-animal-trainer chasing the rumor that some unlikely killer mountain lion was haunting the region of late. Interesting but harmless.

But what he really enjoyed was the fact that these watchful sessions of his up there failed to throw up any sign of gun-toting Truenos showing up in search of a gringo with a yellow hat who'd slain one man and shot up another recently in the Sunstreak Hills.

He supposed he was still vaguely curious about why the gunpackers had jumped him down there. In retrospect, it appeared pretty certain they'd been expecting someone dangerous to come cutting up through the Sunstreaks that night, and had come after him without even taking the trouble first to find out whether he was their man or not.

Their mistake had cost them dear. And while Dulane at least half-expected some kind of retaliation for that half-hour of murderous gunplay, he was vastly relieved when those three days came and went with nothing unusual happening apart from his arrival and some highly suspect big lion sightings to disturb the placid surface of this town's sleepy life.

There was something unique about Limbo which a critic might label terminal apathy, or an admirer extol as a demi-paradise.

The town was a remote and atmospheric blend of Old Mexico and New America, where few ever seemed to move faster than a slow walk, where there was music, indolence and more than a little strangeness to be found amongst the citizens and their customs.

They believed in the occult here, and the palm-reader on the Gibson Street corner was seldom without a customer, he'd noted.

There was a church with its own fat padre and nearby a strange edifice which purported to be a spirit pole whose purpose was to ward off the Evil One, whoever he might be.

And just to add the finishing touch, the broad-bosomed Majestic flowing deeply and silently by, carrying trees and dead dogs and occasionally people away to the South.

Still with his motor revving from Mexico in those first days of sleep-till-noon-and-roister-to-dawn exuberance, Dulane had at first found the town more dead than alive, but then his attitude had softened.

This place seemed to be reaching him, unravelling his knots and sanding down some of his rougher edges, which could, in time, improve his prospects of reaching thirty alive, or so he assured himself. That was a goal he'd felt he was unlikely to achieve barely a month earlier on a storm-raging Diaz City midnight which found him in the bed of a whore who was attempting to do herself in with a gun over some lost love, with himself nursing two bullet burns from his latest gun scrape, an angry mob outside – and just one chance to jump on a horse and hightail it with bullets snarling around his head like a swarm of angry bees.

He sighed. Ahh, they were the days!

Then he frowned soberly.

The hell with high times and midnight run-outs, Dulane. All behind you now you're back in Arizona.

Back in Arizona.

He had to grin with satisfaction.

Up here it felt like he had at last won freedom from those conspirators, grafters, politicos, corrupt Army officials and venal town mayors – all of whom had provided gainful employment for him all winter.

Sure, the money was great and the excitement high. But he knew that a way of life like that could only lead to the grave sooner or later – most likely sooner.

Head back north and live a little before you die, Dulane. That had been his sudden impulse. No dramatic decisions about the future or laments for the past. Just slow down, smell the roses . . . even doze a little in this lofty little cubby-house above the water-tower and dream of . . . what? Nothing specific, drifter. Just having the time and the inclination to drift and dream a little after a full year behind the gun was enough. This was what he'd come searching for, and found. In a place called Limbo.

*

It was good, living easy again. Days, he watched the drowsy routine. He saw the Wells Fargo coach arrive on its weekly run, got to know both the workers and the loaters at the dim bars, came to comprehend how the members of the Pioneer Club fought for something better than Limbo had to offer, yet curiously never seemed to consider quitting to search for someplace else that might offer greater scope for their ideals.

He got drunk with a couple of cowboys bent on a wild weekend, scrupulously avoided opportunities to get involved in the occasional ruckus, observed how Mexican and American families got along together, even heard and smiled tolerantly at something called the Limbo Joke.

It went – so Ellie Palmer told him one twilight when they took a ride down along the river – this way: Question: 'Would you rather be dead or live in Limbo?' Answer: 'There's a difference?'

And he played numbledy-peg with Boy Johnny, was abused by Irish O'Neil after a skinful of rotgut gave the drunk sufficient Dutch courage to speak his mind, wasted a deal of time trying to impress Miss Jean Kelly, was rigidly ignored by the town's number one citizen, Ethan Branson, and had his fortune told by Madame Caspar, who insisted he had a bright future. 'You will find happiness because you are a searcher, *caballero*,' intoned this exotic, world-weary woman, who, like so many others here seemed burdened by the melancholy and submissiveness of the half-life imposed on them in so remote an outpost, yet which at the same time seemed to invest

36

a strange kind of wisdom and spirit in its inhabitants. 'We here in Limbo are searchers no longer. We have searched but have not found . . . which is why we are still here . . . in Limbo, half-way between heaven and hell, as the Bible says, but which I perceive as half-way between living and dying . . .'

Dulane leaned back lazily in his chair and drew deeply on a durham. It was the drowsy mid-afternoon hour on the front porch of the saloon where tables and chairs were set up for those who liked to take a leisurely drink while watching snail-paced life drift by.

At that moment, Madame and Dulane were the Cobweb Palace's sole clientele while the only visible life to be seen upon the street was the dark-garbed Pato family, father, mother and three daughters, all in Spanish black with white collars and cuffs, drifting from store to haberdashers. The Patos were Limbo's oldest family, dating back to well before the arrival of the first Americans. They could have left when the first batch of arrogant gringos arrived, but didn't. Limbo seemed to be populated by people who, despite finding it dull, isolated, heat-stricken and lonesome, still found it more to their liking than anyplace else.

'So, what am I searching for, madame?' he grinned.

'Happiness, of course. What else is there?'

'Hmm, not so sure you're right about that. I mean, what is happiness after all? Is it plenty money . . . *muchos pesos*? Or too many pretty women, mebbe? You'll have to be more specific.'

He winked across the table. Madame Caspar had plainly been a very attractive woman – about a hundred years ago.

'Only teasing, madame. Go on. So I am looking for happiness, eh. Will I find it here?'

'There is no happiness in Limbo. There has not been in seventeen years and never shall be again. Which is why you must not remain here too long, *caballero*, otherwise you will be in danger of becoming just like us.'

Although it suited Dulane to treat his ongoing presence here casually, and with no clear-cut plans in mind for the first time in years, he was curious about where he might be heading, despite himself.

'There's worse things in life than sitting around waiting for something to happen,' he ventured, which was his evaluation of the population of Limbo. He turned sober as he flicked ash from his cigarette. 'There's sleeping with a gun under your pillow every night . . . or celebrating each birthday to the hilt because there's always a strong chance it will be your last.'

He slapped his knees and grinned again.

'But you never know, you could be right about this burg drawing me into its sleepy time-web, madame. I might hang up the guns, grow a little paunch, learn to snap my suspenders and get to be an expert on the weather like the rest of the guys around here. Could do worse.'

'You have the zest for life as I had once, young Dulane. But you should cease risking this great gift with your daring and recklessness, while on the other hand you must never allow yourself to rot away as has been the fate of every man and woman who calls this place home. Somewhere in between these extremes of black and white, there is the place for you, and all you have to do is find it. That will be one dollar.'

He paid and watched her walk away, slipping his dollar into her reticule. She walked lightly like a young woman, this old lady with white hair and creases in her face like canyons.

'Is your life in order now, Mr Dulane?'

The voice came through the window and he turned his head to see Miss Jean standing there, arms folded, dressed more like a schoolmarm than a saloonkeeper, as usual, her serious, heart-shaped face framed by severely drawn-back dark hair.

'You were listening?' he asked.

'No need. Madame told us all yesterday what she thinks of you. She was insistent that she must persuade you to leave before you are sucked into the living death which she claims we all exist in here. She described you as tempestuously vulnerable – whatever that means.'

It took a time for Dulane to get his thinkbox around that one. At last he shrugged. 'Well, like I always say, I'd rather be tempestuously vulnerable than die of the dries.'

She almost smiled. 'I'll get you another.'

He rose and walked inside, where the shutters were closed to create an illusion of coolness. The wheel was still, the lay-outs deserted. And he could feel it; Limbo's atmosphere of time slowed down.

With all urgent needs, desires, ambitions and responsibilities set aside until *mañana.*

'Seems a wise old lady,' he ventured, sliding onto a bar stool, his manner impersonal. Whatever he might have for sale, Miss Jean was definitely not buying, he knew. She had made that plain every time they talked so he didn't knock himself out trying to impress her any longer.

'She isn't old,' she replied, handing him his drink and making change. 'Just looks that way.'

'The town did that to her?'

'In a way.' Jean leaned her elbows upon the bar, almost relaxing in his company for the first time as she gazed out at the hot strip of yellow street visible beneath the batwings.

'She lost her only child in the floods a long time ago. She always claimed the men of the town were too apathetic and cowardly to help save the boy. Perhaps she was right. I was not here then. So she hates the town and every man in it, and you can't live like that without it leaving its mark, I suppose.' He was thoughtful as he sipped his beer. Buried alive in a place like this, then lose your only child? He reckoned that would bring a body down if anything would.

'So, how that lady feels about things in general doesn't bother you any then, Miss Jean?' he ventured after a bit.

She was wiping the bar. He reckoned she could wipe, pour drinks, chat with drunks and keep the girls in line from now till doomsday but would still not look as though she belonged in any saloon. She had quality stamped all over her. He'd known a few quality women in his time, and she was the genuine article. Classy, but 'Limboed', if there was such a word.

'Not really,' she replied. 'Why do you ask, Mr Dulane?'

'Just thinking. Maybe that's the secret of this town's success. Here, you let folks turn hermit, drink, brood about the past, give up or just sit back and watch it all drift by – and nobody gives a damn. That's a rare thing to find anyplace.'

'I'm never sure when you're being complimentary or sarcastic.'

'A bit of both this time, I guess. Not that I'm complaining, but does anything ever happen in Limbo?'

There was irony in the timing of his question. For he was still working on his beer when a commotion outside heralded the arrival on the central block of Ethan Branson, who showed up in his dog-cart in a tweed hunting-suit of the kind affected by gentlemen huntsmen, bringing with him a high-powered rifle, a shotgun and the news that almost succeeded in stirring Chisum Street from its siesta-hour lethargy.

It turned out that Branson, who regularly led some of the Club members out on orderly hunts for antelope and small game in the Gimcrack Hills, had just received a report on yet another sighting of the so-called *La Sombra*. He was inviting whoever might be interested to join him to go after the alleged man-killer, both for the sport and as a precaution against further attacks.

Back out on the porch again, Dulane leaned against the wall with a cigarette jutting from between his teeth, smiling to himself.

Apart from Boy Johnny, who showed up excitedly with his hand-hewn wooden gun to volunteer his services, Branson was receiving no other offers. In other towns, men such as blacksmiths, clerks, depot-hands and shopkeepers might find an opportunity like this irresistibly exciting and stimulating. But this was Limbo where everyone instinctively knew how best to deal with excitement and stimulation of any kind. You sat down until the feeling went away.

'So much for civic-mindedness and responsibility!' snorted Branson, staring from face to face. 'Well, sir, what about you?'

Dulane blinked upon realizing that the imposing citizen was addressing him. Up until now he'd had no dealings with Branson. Far more impressive than his fellow Club members and the population in general insofar as he gave no sign of having succumbed to the general lethargy, Branson, so he'd been warned, disliked and avoided strangers and up until this moment had acted as though unaware of his presence.

'Sorry,' he replied. 'But I make it a policy never to go hunting for unicorns, griffins or pumas the size of bull elephants. Against my religion.'

'What a droll fellow.' Branson's cultivated voice dripped with sarcasm. He raked Dulane up and down with an imperious eye. 'Wouldn't be afraid of something a little out of the ordinary like a killer lion by any chance, would you, Dulane?'

'Buck's not afraid of anything, are you, Buck?'

It was only the kid. But what would he know? Yet for some strange reason that had nothing to with any desire to ride out on a hot day to chase critters, that was exactly what Dulane found himself doing a half-hour later. Volunteering.

Maybe he just wanted to impress the kid? he mused. Or could it be that almost a week of inaction was starting to get to him? He wasn't sure. But he was intrigued when Jean Kelly sought him out and urged him to great caution, should he go up into the hills. The woman insisted that Branson was a wonderful shot and expert huntsman, yet had a reputation for recklessness and high-handedness, which could prove dangerous in the wilds.

Obviously the man in the street also had major reservations about Branson in the field. But after Dulane agreed to ride with Mr Big, another three men seemed reassured enough also to volunteer.

The party struck out at first light next morning.

The Gimcracks lay before them, heat-hazed and lifeless under the slanting heat, as the party travelled north. Dulane reckoned that if they got to scare up a single jackrabbit or a prairie-dog they would be doing well for a heat-stricken day like this, let alone any killer lion.

He puzzled about Jean Kelly and why she had taken the trouble to warn him against going.

CHAPTER 3

DAY OF THE HUNTSMEN

Cheeko Rafer checked his horse and stared backtrail. There it was again. The clatter of hoofs against stone, the low grunting of a horse being forced uphill.

Someone was trailing him across these switchback hills high in the Perros! The Yankee outlaw paled in the shade of his flatbrim. As notorious for his violent rages as for criminal exploits in the Land of the Dons, Rafer tight-reined his mount off the trail into a gaping arroyo that sliced between a bulging spur and an ancient rockslide which was now overgrown with spiny cactus and coarse yellow grass.

His gun was in his fist.

On a good day, Cheeko could draw, shoot, slip the shooter away again and be rolling a cigarette while his victim was still trying to figure out how many bullets had struck him. Leastways, that was what was

44

sometime said of the man now readying yet again for gun trouble, and he knew he was mentally prepared to live up to his reputation should his current assignment lead to gunplay – as many of his enterprises so often did.

There was irony in the situation which found the outlaw leader alone that late afternoon in the Perro Hills, home of the coyote, puma, the great Sonoran buzzard and, off and on, the transient scum and jail-house sweepings of two nations.

Cheeko lived by the gun and it was gun business that had drawn him up from the south. Gun business – and the richest, sweetest lure of all for a man of his nature and record: revenge. Yet despite the fact that he was unrelieved owlhoot scum, he could still be outraged by the very notion that he might be being stalked by another man with his name on a bullet.

The hoofbeats drew closer. His horse showed nervousness and Cheeko smacked it across the ear. He was spitting chips. Bad enough that two men he'd trusted with a serious detail up here had apparently botched things left right and center; now it seemed plain that his henchmen hadn't even secured the trail they knew he'd be following to their rendezvous.

Heads would roll!

Cheeko Rafer was not yet thirty but appeared older because of the treachery lurking in his eyes and the cruelty growing plain around the corners of his mouth. His hat was tilted carelessly on the extreme back edge of his thick, dust-powdered hair. He was an Arizonan who had been down south so long he dressed, smoked, ate and all but thought Mexican.

He lived by the gun and hatreds and feuds were his stock in trade where others might be driven by greed, lust or the quest for glory. He killed better than most, and unless this oncoming horseman ahead turn out to be Wild Bill Hickock himself or Balthazar the Butcher of Caramo Province, laboring his way up through the rocks towards him now, then he was surely on borrowed time. The still unseen horseman kicked his horse into a faster gait as he topped out the climb. Cheeko responded fast, backing his mount into a narrow fissure where man and well-trained horse instantly fell as silent and as immobile as nature's salt-stained 'praying stones' surrounding them, as trouble loomed into sight a short distance along the trail.

A rawboned Mexican with shoulder-length hair and sporting crossed ammunition belts slung across his scrawny chest was intent upon the trail as he came loping by, almost missing the danger lurking on his left.

Almost but not quite.

The Mexican choked out an oath and was sweeping his long-barrelled revolver across his flat belly, his finger already depressing the trigger, when Rafer cut loose.

The American got in the first shot by a fraction, which was usually all the advantage he needed. A leaping spume of yellow-tinted smoke and purple gunflash momentarily shimmered on the fissure walls. The Mexican rider screamed once and was buckling in the middle, stiff-legged and rigid in his spurs with agony, yet still he managed to work his trigger. To no avail.

Calmly, Rafer shot the man twice more through the body then hammered a slug deliberately into the horse as it made to bolt around the corner ahead.

The animal blundered on as straight as though it was running on tram tracks to reach the awful rim of the basin at full clip. Horse and horseman parted company as they became airborne, both last seen screaming and flailing their limbs as they plummeted into the jaws of the mighty chasm below. In the swirl of slow-settling dust Rafer was easing his trembling mount back on to the trail when he caught the drumbeat of yet another set of hoofs. Although appearing calm, the outlaw was raging, less at the unexpected danger he was being forced to deal with than the circumstances which permitted that danger to exist in the first place.

This second manhunter was a fool to keep coming. Had to be. Although the rider must have heard the shooting and screaming, he continued to come on up at headlong speed. Dressed like a dude with a huge sombrero and a gun in either fist, he shouted defiantly as if he expected simply to scare any danger away before him.

Rafer didn't scare.

The instant the Mexican loomed into sight the hardcase's twin guns opened up with a clashing roar that sounded like the hammers of hell and smashed horse and rider down in a roiling dust ball into which the killer continued to pump a fusillade of soft-nosed shells. He went on until his left-hand piece jammed on him and he holstered the second gun and calmly

47

set to work freeing the mechanism. By the time he was through that section of the Perros it had once again become a place of floating dust and deep silences. Rafer ground-tied his mount and picked his way round the slaughtered horse and turned the dead man over with the toe of his boot before going through his pockets. Nothing there to tell a man much of anything. Then, as he perfunctorily slipped a big gaudy ring off a dead finger, he saw the scrolled and embossed letter T upon it, and paled beneath his Mexican bronze.

'Trueno!'

He rippled erect and kicked the corpse in the face. 'You rode for Trueno, you miserable streak of crow-shit . . .' His voice caught and he stared down at the ring again. 'Does this mean Trueno knows?'

Cheeko Rafer was calm again by the time he filled leather and headed on. Like many of his breed the killer credited himself with greater abilities than he actually possessed. His continued survival in one of the most dangerous regions of the borderlands was due partly to luck and partly to his genuine talent for sniffing out danger before it found him and then dealing with it, Colt .45 style.

During recent events involving a bitter enemy of years standing, Cheeko had uncovered a priceless piece of vital information relating to rebel border outlaw Fidel Trueno and someone Rafer hated even more than he did that *bandido* chieftain from the Musketoons. Yet Trueno remained Rafer's most dangerous foe, and upon acquiring certain intelligence against his enemy he had reckoned he had good reason to hope that it could well result in that Spanish butcher's eventual annihilation. At his hands, of course.

But if the unexpected appearance up here of these killers indicated that Trueno had somehow learned what he had set up here in the Perros . . . what might his own chance of survival now be. . . ?

No. He refused to accept it unless reliable henchmen should confirm it. His bunch was expecting him at the Holy Stones.

The trail meandered lazily and lengthily along·like the spoor of a sunstruck sidewinder, but the killer kept to it, riding into a lowering sun. Eventually he reached a lonesome valley and gazed out over barren fields studded by the strange rock pinnacles that from a distance resembled robed figures praying – the so-named Holy Stones. Where five outlaws awaited him.

The outlaws had had time to polish their story. Following Cheeko's orders to the letter, the original seven-man squad comprising almost one third of Rafer's Mexican-based gang, had staked out the Perros to keep watch for Trueno, whom Cheeko had reason to believe would soon arrive there from his Sonoran eyrie.

The bunch had split up to comb the rattlesnake hills and chuckwalla draws aimlessly for days on end before two of them sighted a dangerous-looking intruder making his way north over a week ago now.

They went after him, there was gunplay, one of the bunch was killed and another so badly injured he'd been forced out of the hills to find a good medico. They had fought bravely, so Duvall boasted valiantly, before confessing a little ashamedly that the intruder – singular – had been an American and not a Mexican after all. Definitely not 'a Trueno'.

This was the worst kind of news.

It was touch and go for a while after this as Cheeko Rafer sat on a rock in brooding silence. The outlaws knew the leader was quite capable of losing control and cutting loose in a way they had seen him do before – particularly where Trueno was concerned. Rafer and Trueno went back a long way.

Diaz City and the Palo Pinto region was a lush breeding-ground for criminals and outlaws and the two rivals had fought bloodily for supremacy there for years, while at times occasionally and unwillingly burying the hatchet to fight side by side against their common enemies, namely the Mexican Army and the *Federales*.

Unlike Rafer, who wandered far and wide in his outlawry, Trueno was largely confined to the massive fastness of Musketoon Mountain from which he continued to exert an ever increasing dominance of terror against the rich. He had even launched an ill-starred raid into American territory, resulting in the capture, trial and execution of his two younger brothers.

This event had embittered Trueno and seen him evolve into an even more murderous and unpredictable threat to authority in the region than ever. So much so that Rafer's once wide outlaw territory had been losing influence and revenue ever since, an intolerable situation to which there appeared no feasible solution, until Rafer's diligence produced a lead which suggested that Trueno was preparing to quit his stronghold on a major mission into the north, which surely must leave him exposed and vulnerable.

But had the cat now been let out of the bag? If Trueno knew what Rafer was plotting for him here, might he not change his plans?

'I reckon nobody knows about what happened on the border but Brute and that damn gunslick what shot him up and killed Jagger that night, boss.'

'You reckon!' Rafer's eyes were a bad color as he fingered his sixgun handles and studied his nail-biting *segundos* watching him from a distance. Duvall was pointedly examining the documents that Rafer had, without compuction, lifted from the dead Mexican on the trail.

The brassy stink of uncertainty was still hanging heavily in the air surrounding the Holy Stones when blocky Duvall suddenly jumped to his feet brandishing a piece of bloodstained paper with a tattered .45 hole punched through one corner.

'Everythin's OK, Cheeko old pard,' the man yelled with convincing emotion. He slapped the letter. 'Listen to this.' He read: 'Trueno wishes you and Manuelo to scour the Perros for soldiers or lawmen, and let him know if all is safe.' The man was excited. 'You hear that, Cheeko? They wasn't expectin' to see you, or us. They was just lookin' for lawdogs. Here, take a gander for yourself.'

Cheeko paled. They all feared that Duvall had just

made a blunder. Rafer was illiterate and murderously sensitive about it. But Duvall was taking a huge risk in order to set Rafer's doubts at rest concerning the possibility of Trueno's cancelling his proposed venture into Arizona.

And it worked. Rafer was too relieved to let Duvall's gaffe bother him. What mattered now was that the attack by men under Duvall on some gun-drifter wandering through the hills by night had apparently failed to alert Trueno to his real danger – Cheeko – as he'd feared. And there was every indica-tion – supported by the contents of the letter quoted – that Trueno was still intending to quit his Thunder Mountain fastness and head this way sometime soon.

One thing was for sure. Now that Rafer felt he had been let off the hook he knew he could not afford to leave so important an assignment to underlings. 'Now I'm here I'm taking over personal,' he announced, and there was great relief to see he was no longer stroking his big black guns. 'Reece and Tallinger, you head back south, round up the rest of the bunch and bring them back here. Duvall, you're still in charge of deploying the scouts here to keep watch for the Greaser Brigade, but if you or your clowns make even half of another mistake . . .'

He didn't have to finish. They had been warned.

Nobody noticed that Duvall was lathered in sweat as they got moving. The man had taken a big risk, lying to Cheeko Rafer that way. The letter had been about purchasing a bed-warmer. But his lie had paid off and diverted Cheeko's suspicions.

Duvall was still curious about the identity of that

lone rider who'd killed one of his men and half-crippled another, but the matter was soon forgotten, with any luck for ever.

It was but a short time before hooknosed Reece and big-shouldered Tallinger went dusting away on the long ride back to the city. They rode beneath the same smoking red sun which was spilling over Arizona's Gimcrack Hills fifty miles north.

Ethan Branson said, 'Why are you stopping?'

Dulane did not answer straight away. He had drawn up on a rise of low foothills, turning his head left and right, nostrils flaring. He then studied his horse, observing the way the skin around the nose puckered and twitched occasionally as it rolled its eyes.

'I smell something and the horses do too,' he said. 'Could be cat.'

'Of course it is.' Branson had a way of talking down to people; his tone of voice often implied that another might be talking rubbish or stating the obvious. 'This is mountain lion territory. Didn't I make it clear that's what we'd be looking for? Lions?'

The speaker sat his saddle with military erectness. Out here away from the town, the man appeared just as comfortable and in control as he did playing chess on his house porch with anyone brave enough to take him on. And noting the man's natural assurance along with his air of physical vigor and his authoritarian mannerisms, Dulane found himself reminded afresh that in the sleepy backwater that was Limbo, Branson was definitely the odd man out. While virtually everyone in that town appeared to him to be wounded emotionally, physically or spiritually, Branson alone seemed whole and healthy.

Which made a man wonder: what the hell was he doing buried to hell and gone out here anyway?

'Well, Mr Dulane?'

'Yes, you did say that right enough, Branson,' he conceded. 'But my experience with hunting is that saying you are going after certain game doesn't always mean you are going to find it. So, are you saying because that wood carter says he sighted this killer lion of yours up here that you expect us to flush it, just like that?'

'What I'm saying, sir, is that we know pumas inhabit this rocky section of the hills, which in turn suggests to me that this could well be the area to which this maverick outsider might well gravitate. And you might rein in your hyperboles, if you would be so good. We are discussing a large cat, nothing less but certainly nothing more. Are we ready to continue now?'

Dulane stood reproved. He grinned as he gave his horse its head. He was enjoying this, reminding himself that the last time he had been in rough hill country he'd been fighting for his life in some kind of last-ditch attempt by Mexico to make him pay for his sins before allowing him to escape to Arizona. Hunting mountain lions, regular or outsize, certainly beat hunting men or being hunted. He could testify to that.

The winding trail was climbing away from sage and mesquite and prickly pear cactus towards the piñon shelves. The day was still hot but cooling a little as they went higher, the still air crystal-clear.

Branson led the way with Dulane coming next and the rest a short distance behind. Two of the men were the storekeeper and the Wells Fargo agent, dues-paid members of the Pioneer Club who hunted regularly with Branson. They gave the impression that they were up here only because Branson expected it, that hunting was not a genuine interest for either of them. And that went double for hunting killer lions.

The remaining towers seemed keen enough but were still acting a little jittery as they stared round at the widely spaced trees on either side of the trail which now meandered across a wide, reddish clay bank.

This was the transitional area between the desert and the higher zones. Piñon and juniper were beginning to appear here and there, along with scrub oak and the occasional tamarisks. Although a man of the southwestern plains, Dulane liked the high country. He liked to hunt too, when he got the chance, realized just how long it was since he'd climbed hills for fun, not simply in order to get from one place to another. He had started out hunting animals like every Western boy but in time had become more expert at hunting men. Now he was back to the animals. It felt good and he guessed he had Limbo to thank.

Doc Belden drew abreast, looking hot and uncomfortable in jacket, tie and derby hat. The medico was a Pioneer, a gentle, weary looking little man whom Dulane nonetheless found intelligent and friendly.

The doctor was reported to be something of an expert on the flora and fauna of Yellow Desert.

'Hot day, Doc.'

'Yes, but cooler up here above the desert, Mr Dulane.' The little man gazed around. 'I must say I'm glad you volunteered today. Ethan would have been put out had I failed to accompany him, but I'm a coward and don't mind admitting it. He is an excellent shot but no real huntsman as I understand the term. You, on the other hand, are quite expert, I'm sure.'

Dulane negotiated his way round a clump of gray-colored brush.

'What makes you say that, Doc?'

'Just your style, I suppose. You give the impression you don't fear anything.'

'Well, I can tell you that's just an impression. I get scared of lots of things . . . but not about cats as big as cows, luckily.'

'I sense you don't believe what is being said about this lion?'

'You'd be right.'

'Then might I ask why you agreed to come?'

'Lots of reasons, Doc,' Dulane replied, looking ahead. 'One was the need for a little action. A man needs something to burn up his energy.'

'Ahh, yes, I can remember when I had energy . . .'

Dulane suppressed a grin. The slope-shouldered medico conveyed the impression that he had never hopped, jumped, skipped or felt energy's insistent pulsebeat in a lifetime. Which made him an ideal citizen in go-slow Limbo, where energy seemed almost a hindrance.

56

'The last time we hunted lion up here, Ethan's mount took fright and threw him, breaking his leg. I did not think he would be anxious to go puma-hunting again, although I suppose I'm partly responsible for that.'

'They tell me you're the one most responsible for these fairy tales about *La Sombra*, Doc?'

'Oh, that animal's no fiction, Mr Dulane. The information we receive on the beast may well be exaggerated some, but it definitely exists and is much larger than normal.'

'Oh yeah?' Duval's skepticism was obvious. 'And how would you account for that?'

Doc Belden was almost patronizing as he replied.

'The interbreeding between the mountain lion or puma, and the jaguar of the south is rightly regarded as rare but certainly not unknown, Mr Dulane. Such matings have been well documented by science, and in Tucson I once saw the progeny of such a liaison in a small, unusual cub which unfortunately died before reaching adulthood. But it was certainly outsized for its age.'

'You're going to tell me this *La Sombra* did survive to adulthood, though?'

'The first I heard of this animal was in Sonora where a big young female panther with the larger head of a jaguar's shape, killed some cattle and was shot and wounded by *vaqueros*. Amongst the hunters that day was a scout for a circus searching for animals for the ring, and he was able to establish beyond reasonable doubt that the creature was almost certainly half-lion, half-jaguar. Ever since, there have been sightings of this so-named *La Sombra* as it worked its way northwards, but it did not really come to prominence until the killing of two range riders on the Rafter K Ranch this side of the border a month ago—'

'Mountain lions don't attack men,' Dulane cut in.

'Jaguars do. An eye-witness to that incident insisted the killer was a female panther, much larger than an average puma male.'

'And now it's come to scare us here?'

'According to a couple of possible sightings — yes. Charlie Tom the mailrider swears he sighted a big female and a much smaller male crossing the Silverton trail just on dusk four nights ago. He said it looked big and mean enough to eat his horse.' Doc Belden smiled. 'But don't worry, I can understand your doubts.'

Dulane let it go at that and moved off to the west of Branson who was now travelling with Dingus the blacksmith. There was a resinous smell up here where a layer of brown conifer needles covered the ground. Bars of sunlight angled down through the trees and dappled the earth. The going grew steeper and Dulane held back to allow Branson and the blacksmith to take the narrowing trail ahead of him.

The puma must have been hiding amongst the rocks, anticipating that the party might veer away. Instead the riders were coming directly towards it. It burst from the rocks and trees a bare hundred feet distant in a tawny, blurring flash to streak across broken ground as rifles came up and excited shouts rang across the hillside. The beast travelled in great bounds, contracting to small then stretching out to its full coil-spring length before coiling once again.

Dingus cut loose first, his bullet spanging close, causing the lion to change direction. It was a fatal mistake. Branson now had time to draw a bead. He triggered twice. The animal skidded in dust, spun and fell with a scream of pain, biting at its side. Before it could rise other rifles were thundering and it was quickly over.

The dead animal was no giant, merely an average-sized mountain lion full of bullet holes. Its appearance was normal apart from a blaze of white on the forehead, which Doc Belden found of interest.

'The mailrider described the two lions he saw on the trail the other night,' he told Branson, who was looking acutely disappointed by their kill. 'Said the male had a white blaze, just like this.'

'Does that mean,' Dulane asked dubiously, 'that as well as having a mankilling panther about we now have one that's lost its mate and who will therefore likely be ornerier and meaner than ever?'

'It could be, sir,' Belden replied uneasily as he gazed round at the dark and silent trees. 'Yes . . . that might very well yet prove to be the case.'

'Wrong,' declared Dulane, sounding sure. 'This here is your mysterious giant critter. You nailed it and the fun is over. Don't you agree, Branson?'

Branson sighed as he leaned upon his rifle, studying the animal at his feet. 'I'm afraid you could be right . . . but I'd very much prefer you addressed me as mister.'

'That's OK, Mr Branson,' Dulane replied. 'So long

as you remember I'm Mr Dulane.'

Branson didn't like that but Buck's hard stare made sure he would not forget it. Then Doc Belden came between them and spread skinny arms wide.

'No bickering, friends,' he urged. 'Perhaps we didn't quite get the monster we came after but we've sure enough bagged a very fine catch. And should this prove to be the mankiller then I rather think this calls for a celebration, don't you?'

'Of course you're right, Doctor,' said Branson. 'And a celebration we shall have. Er, you will pardon my unintended rudeness of a moment ago, Mr Dulane?'

'Forgotten,' Dulane replied. He didn't carry petty grudges. Branson was a gentleman, obviously. But now, as he would do again, he could not help wondering exactly what kind of gentleman that might be. The man who was obviously the power and driving force behind Limbo seemed more and more obviously to be the only one who didn't even remotely seem to fit in such a backwater.

CHAPTER 4

BANDIDO

The Diaz City realtor was a rich and cultivated hidalgo with some strange ideas and even stranger acquaintances. To his grand hacienda atop the highest hill in town, all manner of radicals, revolutionaries and anti-government extremists gathered from time to time, while the law turned a blinkered eye. The don was far too rich and powerful for the *teniente* to interfere with. And besides – or so the law office reasoned – he never actually broke their laws, simply played host to some who did.

So it was possible for the authorities to justify their inaction where this hidalgo was concerned, in return for which consideration the don contributed generously to many causes and – as was so often stated in his defence – kept his hands clean while continuing to enjoy the company of some whose hands may have never been clean since birth.

It was only the second occasion upon which the

don had dared have the *bandido* chieftain from Musketoon Mountain cross his threshold. Strict secrecy was observed that night. For even the don who might occasionally entertain certain hairy and wild-eyed gentlemen given to blowing up government trains and preaching open rebellion in public places, might not be forgiven for playing host to Fidel Trueno.

No way could Trueno be passed off as political, misguided or an enemy of the state in name only. He was a brigand, a badman, a butcher and murderous son of a whore who had no interest in whoever might be in government providing they didn't interfere with his criminal activities.

But if this were the case, why did the don dare have such a one to his hacienda with all the attendant risks and uncertainties that such a visit might entail?

The answer was simple.

The don was fascinated and intrigued by men who went out and actually did all the lawless and dangerous things he only dreamed or talked about doing. He might be rich, honored and respected but he got his thrills by fraternizing with the darker side of the law and politics.

At first glance Fidel Trueno seemed little different from any other handsome and self-assured *renegado* with the look of the wide open spaces about him along with considerable charm and natural grace.

He arrived that night with just two companions-cum-bodyguards, large silent men who watched everyone carefully with unblinking eyes and who were never more than a step or two from the leader's side.

There were other guests in attendance but it was obvious from the start that Trueno was the star attraction. For this was the outlaw-brigand who had successfully defied the authorities of the province both before and since an historic crime-spree in the United States during which Trueno had lost two brothers to the hangman's noose.

The wealthier and more respectable guests might well be appalled by this man's reputation but this only served to enhance the fascination he exerted over them in the early part of the evening, before their host eventually showed them all the gate in order to enjoy the stimulating company of this wild and notorious one alone.

Don Luis Lopez had heard rumors and counter rumors of events involving his guest, upon whom he was relying to either confirm or deny them. Merely being privy to what was taking place in alien circles enabled the hidalgo to absorb the thrill and dangers of the outlaw life without risking one hair of his fine silver mustache in the process.

The attraction for Trueno in a meeting such as this was that he got to rub shoulders with the aristocracy and soak up their perverted admiration. And, as was often the case, to receive support and actual funding from the discontented upper classes, many of whom might secretly wish that someone like Trueno would one day grow powerful enough to overthrow Madrid-funded authority altogether so that they could replace it with the infinitely more brutal but profitable mastery of the rich.

What Lopez was mainly interested in tonight was the whispered report he'd gleaned that had his guest about to leave his mountain stronghold to visit America again. That was something Trueno had vowed never to do again following the death by hanging of his brothers Manuel and Miguel in Amarillo, Texas, a fate Fidel himself had only averted by staging a daring last-minute escape from Ranger headquarters.

Was the report really true? Lopez wanted to know. And if so, what had caused Trueno to change his mind? For was it not a fact that the American authorities were still hunting him two years after his escape and would be for the rest of his life? What possible reason could tempt him to set foot on gringo soil again – as some were whispering he would?

To his astonishment, Trueno told him. The duplicitous Lopez leaned back in his fine chair, nodding his silver head in admiration and something like awe. True, true, he must agree. What Trueno had confided sounded like reason enough.

The host had planned for the evening to run much later, yet soon found reason to bring it to an end. He was smiling graciously as he shook hands with the lithe and handsome outlaw on the lamplit portico, stood waving as the party with the aura of the wild places surrounding them vaulted onto their horses and were gone like ghosts into the night.

Only then was this depraved old dabbler in the sick underside of the way of life that had made him rich, seen to sag at the knees and needed assistance to make it back inside, where brandy was called for.

Until tonight Lopez had always enjoyed his hobby of entertaining rogues from time to time, even counting some as friends. But he had not enjoyed the last part of tonight's visit, however. Indeed it had scared him to realize that any man could be so filled with hatred and obsessed by revenge as Fidel Trueno, to such a degree that he considered the *bandido* to be half crazy.

And told himself it was foolish for a man like himself to have any connection at all with such a one, even if he might enjoy it. For surely any man as viciously unstable as handsome Trueno could just as easily turn upon him, should the mood suddenly take him, for whatever reason.

He almost felt a twinge of genuine sympathy for the gringo whose hiding-place had finally been uncovered by the killer. But of course he would not lift a finger to warn this man any more than he would alert the American authorities that one of their most wanted *renegados* would soon be slipping across their borders. Instead he would do as he had always done and look after himself, Don Luis. Unsuspecting Arizona's looming dangers on the epic scale were its own, and it was welcome to them.

The ancient river-rat readily accepted such phenomena as ghosts, spirit people and the ability to predict a man's life span simply by studying the grounds in his coffee-mug. When someone had lived man and boy better than eighty years along the sometimes bone-dry river-bed, the sometimes roaring torrent that was the Majestic River, which meandered its broad and lazy route southwestward just a little south of the town, a man saw and experienced many things that logic or knowledge could not explain away.

Once, many years earlier, he'd awakened at midnight in his riverbank shack to peer out and see a ghostly raft with vaporous figures on board go drifting by upon the Majestic's stately bosom, waving their arms and screaming silently for help. To discover a little while later that such a party had drowned upriver at Tanner's Bend a week earlier.

He'd made the mistake of telling people in Limbo about that remarkable experience. Everybody scoffed. Their mockery ensured that ever after he kept his own counsel, never mentioning the transparent weeping woman in widow's black whose team of soundless black-plumed horses carried her by along the river trail maybe once or twice a year.

There were others, of course. The 'Shadow People' he called them; the no-longer living, but real, intensely real to his old eyes.

Sometimes he welcomed their eerie visits as a counter to his lonesomeness, other times they disturbed him. The old man had an uneasy hunch that another visitation might be due that night of the puma hunt. He was fearing he'd been alone too long this time to endure the company of the shades. So he decided to shave, wash and head into Limbo for the hunt party they were throwing to commemorate the killing of the 'giant' lion – and allow the ghosts to have the run of the river tonight if they wanted.

66

But of course, being solitary by nature, he hadn't been rubbing shoulders with noisy towners an hour before he was regretting his decision. Even so, he stayed on and surprised himself by almost having an enjoyable time of it, or at least up until the moment when the fun was cut short in a way that almost scared even him.

Jean Kelly lived alone.

In a place like Limbo where men heavily outnumbered women, and real ladies were rare as stardust, this was a matter of choice rather than circumstance. Despite the fact that she was almost thirty and settling into the primness of early spinsterhood, she had a string of admirers any one of whom would readily rescue her from the terrible fate of old maidhood in return for just an encouraging smile.

Indeed she had received no fewer than three invitations to tonight's hunt party before leaving the saloon at dusk; two from regulars and the other from the hero of the lion-hunt himself, Mr Branson.

Occasionally Jean accepted an invitation from Branson, who had actually proposed several times during his two years in town. She had declined, graciously she hoped, on each occasion and knew she would continue to do so.

She had fallen in love once, and that was enough. He had left her for someone more vivacious, lively and less melancholy. That was in Utah. A short time later she said goodbye to her family and boarded a stage. She did not have a destination, had no idea where she might settle with her life's savings. Until the Wells Fargo's Arizona Express coach stopped for a horse-change at a town along the longest and lonesomest stretch of border trail, and suddenly her destination had a name after all. It was Limbo.

Stroking her hair with a mother-of-pearl brush by her window as she gazed out, Miss Jean knew she had never regretted her decision to settle here, doubted she ever would.

For if there was one unarguable verity in this ordered, predictable life which she led here on the fringes of the Yellow Desert, it was that this town was made for people like her and her friends.

For the lonely, the seekers, the breaking ones and the broken ones. The people whom life had damaged in some way, yet who were not ready to disintegrate into drink or dissolution. People who wished to go on living, but away from the demands and expectations and everyday pain of places where one was always expected to want more, more, then much more after that.

In Limbo you could settle for less of everything and no one thought any the worse of you. You could grab for success if you wished, drown yourself in whiskey, have a baby to a Navajo raider chieftain or own a saloon, even as a woman.

The only sin in Limbo was not to recognize the town for what it really was, and respect it as such. And what that something was, was the End of the Line, a place most could not leave behind quickly enough but which people like Miss Jean identified as Home at first glance.

'Hi, Miss Jean.'

The woman started. Admittedly she had been dreaming a little, but had seen nobody. Then she saw a large, partly eaten pie rise up beyond the sill to catch the light spilling from her window. Astonished, she leaned forward to make out the boy's smiling face as he continued to hold his pie aloft for her admiration.

'Boy Johnny! Where on earth did you get that?'

The child lowered the pie-plate to the sill and stood on the garden border to reach her level.

'Buck bought it for me,' he grinned. Then he frowned. 'Unk's drunk again. You look real pretty tonight, Miss Jean.'

The woman's face was blank. She had grown skilled at concealing her feelings, so skilled in truth that it was beginning to show in the tight lines at the corners of her mouth and the frown of self-discipline beginning to mar the smoothnes of her brow. Mostly her feelings remained well under control but occasionally a shaft penetrated her armour. This street-urchin touched her heart, yet she always fought against it. That was what bona fide Limbo citizens did as a matter of course: 'Keep emotion at arm's length and it will never snap back and hurt you.' That could have been their tenet to live by.

'Thank you, Johnny. And I'm sure that was very generous of Mr Dulane.' Then she heard herself ask, 'Is he attending the celebration, do you know?'

'Guess so,' replied the child, taking a bite of the pie. He chewed vigorously. 'Leastways he was brushing his hair and putting on perfume when I took his change back to him.'

'Perfume? You mean lavender-water, don't you? Gentlemen don't wear perfume.'

'I guess that's what I mean,'

Someone called from across the street. Jean leaned out to see a group of her fellow Pioneer members standing and waving. There was Doc, Henri the Painter, Louis Dundee the former peace officer, Agent Dayton and of course Branson looking resplendent in a dark broadcloth suit.

'Coming, Jean?' called Doc Belden.

'I'll be along presently,' she called back. 'You all look very smart. I shan't be long, you go ahead.'

The child's attention flickered between his pie and the receding group. The whole affair of the lion-hunt and kill excited him, as did the impromptu party to celebrate the success. While opinion on whether or not the dead puma was the mankiller from the Rafter T was divided; Johnny was convinced it was, his only regret being that he had not been in at the kill. This he confided to the woman as she finished her grooming, yet Jean was barely listening as she drew her lace stole about her shoulders, turned down the light, then came out onto the porch to join him.

'What does he talk about, Johnny?' she asked abruptly.

He brushed crumbs from his shirt-front, puzzled. 'Who, Miss Jean?'

'Mr Dulane, of course. You two seem to get along very well. What sort of things do you discuss with him? What does he tell you about himself?'

Johnny frowned as they started down the garden

path. 'Well, we talk a lot about hunting and fishing and suchlike.'

'No, I mean about himself. For instance, does he ever say where he comes from, or when he intends leaving Limbo? Things like that?'

'He talks about Mexico a lot.'

'Oh? Does he speak about . . . family?'

'I asked him if he is married and he says he's always been too busy.'

'I see.' Jean did not realize that she was smiling until the boy spoke again.

'Does that make you happy, Miss Jean? Knowing Buck's not married, that is?'

'Of course not. Why should it?' Miss Jean was her sober self again as she reached down and took the child's hand. 'Come along, we must not be late. And don't you think you might discard that gun while you are eating?'

Johnny fumbled awkwardly with his wooden rifle. 'But I'm a hunter, Miss Jean. Just like Buck. And if Buck never shot the lion, I would have.'

'Mr Dulane did not shoot the lion – Mr Branson did.'

'So they say. I'll bet Mr Branson paid him to say that.'

Miss Jean compressed her lips but did not speak, as the first strains of music drifted from the tiny town hall up ahead. She felt eager for the evening, and this puzzled her. It was a long time since she had been genuinely eager about anything.

It was eleven o'clock before Irish O'Neil was ejected for

71

falling over once too often, then well past midnight before the revellers permitted the three-man orchestra to take a break from supplying dance-music for the dozen or so couples cramming the tiny floor.

Ethan Branson, perspiring from his dancing exertions, seized the opportunity to call for quiet in order that he might make a formal announcement regarding the killing of the lion, which after all was the reason Limbo was taking one of its rare opportunities to enjoy itself.

Although not overlooking the assistance of his 'fellow huntsmen', the speaker dealt with them cursorily before taking considerably more time to dramatize the hunt itself and the core role he'd played in bringing down the 'killer lion'.

Seated near the punchbowl at the long, cloth-covered table with Ellie from the Cobweb Palace, Dulane swabbed his brow and grinned as Branson laid claim to putting paid to *La Sombra*, while at the same time acknowledging guardedly that the puma he shot might not have been the mankiller at all.

This took some doing, and he was forced to admire the way the big man juggled his words to convey an impression without actually nailing himself down. This man would make a good lawyer, he thought, if they had lawyers here.

He was realizing only belatedly that he was having a damn good time. This surprised him. Almost as much as did the realization that he was still here long after he'd expected to be gone. What could it be about Limbo that was keeping him away from bigger places such as Cromwell and Tacey where an *hombre* like himself could really get to howl at the moon at full volume in the company of men and women cut from his own cloth.

Instead he found himself cutting country jigs with a saloon-girl, executing sober waltz steps with the saloon-girl's boss-lady, trading jokes with Doc Belden and helping conceal Boy Johnny when his uncle was after him to clip him round the ears.

Heck! He was even enjoying listening to Branson build himself up as the Arizonan Jim Bridger, until the crowd began to grow restless and the orchestra, refreshed and restored, returned to the podium ready to resume. Was he still recovering from the rigors of the southland? Or was it remotely possible that he was actually simply enjoying himself in Noplace, Nowhere County, Arizona?

Then suddenly he found himself looking at Jean Kelly just as it seemed she turned to gaze in his direction.

He felt a tingle run down his spine and was astonished. He was a great admirer of women but he rarely tingled. So he took a second look and next moment was on his way across the polished floorboards to invite her to dance.

She agreed. She seemed remote and distant at first but he was astonished how quickly this attractively prim and proper woman really didn't have any inhibitions about dancing with a gunfighter, as he might have expected.

And a curious thought entered his head. Was he still a man of the gun? Or had he changed since coming to Limbo and doing a lot of deep thinking?

Stranger things had happened, he supposed.

When he realized it was the supper dance he invited her to join him and the next half-hour simply flew until it was time to resume dancing, and the fiddler was tuning up his strings when they all heard it.

At first they thought it was the fiddle, until it quickly established itself as such a sound as few had ever heard before.

It was a long, quivering howl of pain and anger, mournful and menacing, which seemed to come floating down from the hills to enter that room and spread its chill among the dancers like the hand of fear touching every face. It rose and fell by turns, filling the spaces, causing people to stare at one another in mounting unease as someone whispered, 'Mountain lion,' and someone else added, 'Surely that ain't no reg'lar panther!'

Soon there began a nervous shuffling of feet and a clearing of throats, a sudden burst of forced, jittery laughter. A group of youths by the door began talking loudly as though to display their bravado. Yet so chillingly dreadful was that primitive scream that long before it choked off at last in a terrifying snarl of wrath, the entire room, perhaps the whole town, had gone silent again.

Somehow it didn't seem possible to speak until the last eerie note quivered away into moonlit distance and was lost.

Voices murmured, rose, began to hum as everyone began moving about, looking a little shamed now that, for a time, they had been so fearful.

Then the boozy voice of the blacksmith came loudly as he spoke with shaky conviction:

'Well, Mr Branson sir, guess that settles the question 'bout whether your puma was one you went after or not.' Though red-faced and weaving, the man was yet somehow very convincing as he jerked a thumb in the direction of the hills. 'I ain't never sighted it, and mebbe I never will . . . but that was *La Sombra*, Mr Branson – you try and tell me it wasn't.'

Everyone stared expectantly at Branson. Just the way he looked as he drew a kerchief from the breast pocket of his fine broadcloth jacket to dab at his temples told them he was not going to attempt to rebut the man's words. That he could not do.

CHAPTER 5

TRACKS

Once clear of town Dulane headed out west along the
Majestic. It was just after first light and the world was
still sleeping. A low mist clung to the water, and as he
paused to roll and light his first cigarette, Madame
Caspar and her long-ago drowned child came to
mind. Last night, late, when they had danced, he had
found that strange woman bright, vivacious and looking much younger than on the day when she had first
hinted at the great tragedy of her life.

Then, just as the dance was ending, Boy Johnny
came up to them and made them both laugh by
shooting them with his carved pistol.

'What a kid,' he'd remarked as the child scooted
away.

'How old is he?'

'Three and a half.'

Madame frowned pensively. 'Are you sure? He
appears older?'

Dulane shrugged.

'Well, so Miss Jean tells me . . .'

'He was three and a half . . . when the river took him . . .'

'Huh?'

'My son. His name was Daniel . . .'

'Must be mighty hard to see another kid like Boy Johnny, then. I mean, missing your kid, and all.'

He was astonished to see her eyes twinkling as she gazed back over all those years. 'Oh, not really. He comes to see me often.'

'Huh?'

She squeezed his hand, then let it drop. 'It is all right, young man, I'm not crazy, as many say.' She made a curiously graceful gesture embracing the crowded room. 'He's here tonight. Of course he's older now, just seventeen. But he loves the town and especially the young. He will be charmed by Boy Johnny and we shall talk of him later. We have such lovely talks . . .'

Dulane grinned reflectively and shook his head. She was crazy, of course, but damnably convincing. For a moment or two at the dance he'd almost believed he could see a seventeen-year-old kid watching his mother from the sidelines, so clearly and convincingly did she speak of him.

The horse ran freely as he cut for higher ground, putting the big river well behind him. Although thin mist still clung to the semi arid lands south of the desert, the distant hills of Mexico, the Perros, stood out clearly in the pearly light.

There were dead men over there to the south, and

badmen who would murder a man on sight. He no longer worried about being trailed up here by whatever breed of heller he'd tangled with that first night across the border. Which, he supposed, left him with one less reason for staying on.

Until now he'd not been prepared simply to ride on and perhaps leave Limbo saddled with trouble of his making, should there be badmen coming after him for blowing that hardcase to glory. Nothing was really holding him back now . . . or was there something? Maybe there was . . . and that was surely something unexpected to occupy his thinking on a fine day such as this.

Soon he was in the Gimcracks, the horse laboring as they climbed a tree-dotted incline just as the sun burst loose of the eastern rim.

Just a quick check around, Dulane, so he advised himself. He didn't want to make more of last night's feral scream than it warranted, but knew he would feel better if he took a look around before . . .

Before what, Dulane? You are thinking of quitting, aren't you? Admit it. He had to concede this was so. He was still amazed he'd stayed on this long or enjoyed it so much. But now restlessness was prodding at him, urging him to make a decision. There was nothing for him here even if at times he might have almost convinced himself otherwise. Maybe he liked some of the people here, could be he liked one or two a lot. But they had survived without him before as they surely would again.

And yet this nagging feeling of responsibility was something he must confront and shake . . .

Boy Johnny, Miss Jean . . . They were really strong people in their own right who didn't need a footloose gunfighter cluttering up their lives. *Right, Dulane? Right!*

He knew he would miss that kid, but was amazed and even shaken up a little to realize just how much he might also miss Miss Jean. Could it be that at long last he had. . . ?

'No way!' he said aloud and the horse pricked its ears at the sudden sound of his voice.

He rode on.

Needle beds muffled the sound of the horse now as he headed on for the kill site. The days were shortening. Ravens cawed and fluttered from branch to branch ahead of him in yellow-leafed trees. The hills' high crests climbed into a luminous sky.

All this the rider was aware of, but only peripherally. He rode with sharply narrowed eyes and a free hand resting on his gunbutt.

That scream last night. He'd not heard anything like that since the gunrunning operation down in the jungles of Quamago.

They'd carted the carcass of the lion back to town the previous night. He found the kill site covered with the tracks of men and horses.

There was a set of fresher tracks that belonged to neither.

Dulane squatted on his spurs to study pug-marks bigger than his fist. This critter had come in from the west, circled several times, then vanished in the rocks to the north of the glade.

He was massaging the back of his neck as he

prowled about, sniffing and listening. He knew he had not wanted to find something like this; hoping that what had been heard last night had been magnified and exaggerated by distance, climatic conditions, anything but the suspicion that it had come from the throat of a really big cat.

This was the spoor of such a cat.

'Seems I owe you an apology, Doc . . .'

Swinging up, he started off. The freshness had gone from his face as he made for the trail, and his cigarette had no taste. Seemed he'd barely reached his decision to quit Limbo before he was forced to think again. Was it right for a man to involve himself in something which might in time bring danger upon a town that had shown him hospitality, then simply up and hightail it? Had he ever really understood what responsibility meant?

Passing under heavy oaks he listed aloud the various destinations he could be heading for by midday, along with the names of 'close friends', mostly female, who would surely be glad to see Buck Dulane step down at their door.

He was up to Marilyn from Friday Wells when a shadow flickered across the clay before him and he jerked his head up to see the buzzard planing overhead on a northeastern flight course, slowly vanishing behind the trees.

He followed its course.

They rose in a raucous dark cloud twenty minutes later when he rode into the clearing, flapping away with awkward heavy wingbeats, cruel beaks dripping red.

The scavengers had only just got started on the fallow deer lying by the jackpine with claw and beak, and were as yet to inflict much damage. But something had all but ripped the animal in half without apparently eating any of it. Something that left big, fist-sized prints in the surrounding soft earth.

From his window, Ethan Branson watched the Wells Fargo coach slowly gathering speed as it left the depot and the central block behind in a cloud of dust to begin the long haul westward to the next town.

It was an accepted fact of life in Limbo that Branson was never part of the regular crowd that gathered at the depot to make something of an occasion of the Line's once-weekly arrival and departure. He was, after all, a man of great importance and style, who seemed to feel that standing around waiting for a coach to come or go was beneath his dignity, and this was understood by all.

The town's leading citizen had other qualities and habits that also set him apart. He read and wrote a great deal, and it was rumored that his library room was stocked with leather-bound volumes all to do with the law. He received newspapers from Texas every week on the Wells Fargo coach, yet never received or posted any mail.

Madame Caspar insisted there was an aura of mystery surrounding Ethan Branson which she alone could on occasion plainly detect. She sometimes utilized her cards and symbols in an attempt to probe his background, but with little success, although more than once she had confided to believers that there was both 'blood and power' in his past.

None of which, of course, disturbed Ethan Branson as he continued to read, ride, walk, hunt and enjoy the company of his fellow members of the Pioneer Club which he himself had moulded from the thin upper-crust of Limbo society. After the stage was gone, he slipped on his favorite English tweed jacket, collected hat and Irish thornstick from the hallway rack and set out on his morning constitutional.

For reasons nobody could begin to guess, this meager scatter of buildings making up an outpost of civilization that was the merest flyspeck of life in the desolate heart of the vast desert lands, was unfailingly attractive and reassuring to this man who had spent the greater part of his life in big cities surrounded by prominent and stimulating people who courted and deferred to him.

In reality, Madame Caspar's 'blood and power' background which she attributed to him was uncannily close to the mark, but her powers were not strong enough to enable her to dig any deeper. Had they been, she would have uncovered enough that was startling and even alarming. She might even have divined that the factors most responsible for Ethan Branson's puzzling ongoing tenure here in nowhere town were fear and secrecy.

Perhaps those who knew him best might realize that there was much which appeared to be secretive about this isolated, arrogant man, but fear was certainly not an emotion one would associate with him.

As was sometimes his habit on his strolls, Branson dropped in on several of his fellow Club members. He took coffee with former Sheriff Dundee, collected his Texas newspapers from Mick Dayton at the depot, eventually made his way along to the Cobweb Palace and took a cup of powerful black coffee with Jean Kelly. It was possible that Branson was in love with the serious-minded Miss Jean. He could not be sure because she never permitted him to draw close enough to find out. There was no doubting her attractiveness and intelligence. But although she was the only citizen he regarded as remotely close to a genuine equal, and upon whom he danced attendance at every opportunity, he was kept at arm's length, regrettably never seemingly more so than now.

And Ethan Branson suspected that he knew the reason for this distancing between them, as he made his seemingly casual enquiry now. 'Has our friend Dulane left town yet, Miss Jean?'

'I'm sure I wouldn't know, Ethan. Why do you ask?'

'I'd prefer he did go, don't you know. Unsettling influence, a fellow like that.'

'He's very popular.'

'With certain elements, no doubt.' He raised powerful dark eyebrows quizzically. 'I couldn't help but notice you danced with him on several occasions last evening.'

'He dances well.'

She was so controlled and composed that at times he felt he wanted to shake her. There was sadness in

83

Jean Kelly's past, and like himself, Branson knew she had found both peace and escape from this here in Limbo. The impression she conveyed to him was that of an attractive young woman strangely willing to take on the mantle of middle-aged spinsterhood just as quickly as she might. Yet another and far more disturbing impression for him, was that of a vulnerable, romantic woman who, although protected and armoured by self-discipline, was just waiting for the day when some gallant would come storming into her life and carry her away.

He wished that hero might be himself, yet feared it could one day turn out to be some flashy, muscular and probably shady character – just like Buck Dulane.

Branson left shortly afterwards and Jean rose to collect their cups and saucers.

'You can come out now,' she said, and a toy rifle parted drapes screening the alcove in back as the boy emerged. Jean was stern with him. She often was with people she feared might grow too close to her. 'Why did you hide from Mr Branson when he arrived?'

'I thought it might be Irish.'

'No you didn't. You dislike Mr Branson because he comes calling on me, do you?'

'He calls me a brat. I hate him.'

Her face softened. There were welt marks on Boy Johnny's neck where his drunken uncle had beaten him with something. Broke her heart to see how a dog of a man treated an angel of a child. But she would not let her defences down. 'It's not right to hate, child.'

'Buck says he hates people who beat up little kids.'

The woman paused on her way to the bar.

'You like Mr Dulane very much, don't you, Johnny?'

'I wish he was my dad.'

'We can't always have what we wish for.'

'I wish he was my dad and you were my mom. Then we could have fun. Like, hunt the big lion together.'

For reasons he could not begin to understand – nor she herself for that matter – Miss Jean sent him scooting, and it was a scowling and unhappy child who almost collided with the woman on the plankwalk as he made his way towards the billiard parlor.

Madame Caspar tousled his thick hair and smiled in a way that stripped years from her face. 'Ah, my darling little one. Why so unhappy on such a fine morning?'

But Johnny pulled away and hurried off, bare brown legs twinkling. He mostly avoided Madame, yet for the very opposite reason he avoided people like Ethan Branson. She was overly kind and solicitous, and that could scare him almost as much as folks acting strange.

'Poor little mite,' Madame lamented to the blacksmith passing by. 'The way he has to live! I fear something terrible may befall him some day.'

The blacksmith shook his head and moved on, leaving Madame twisting her hands and watching the child vanish down a laneway, taking his aura with him. Her strange gifts had been bequeathed to

85

Madame the day she lost her child in the great flood. She had not understood them at first, only knew her new strengths were genuine. Of course, her foresight and predictions were not always accurate; she didn't expect them to be. But there were times when her clairvoyance operated so strongly and clearly that it was almost frightening. Today was such a day.

Boy Johnny's aura today was one of danger; she could see it hovering over him like dark wings. And upon rising when she had first looked north at the Gimcracks, Madame had felt menace emanating from the distance-blued ranges like a physical push. And now, to confuse and depress her even more on such a fine morning she was receiving the same alarming vibrations coming from the south in the direction of the border.

Madame could not recall any time when so many strong and unpleasant influences seemed to be directed at her town at the same time. She decided to go home and pray she might be wrong. Only time would reveal whether, with these inexplicable gifts which might have been granted her to compensate for the loss of her infant son, Madame's instinctive warnings about Boy Johnny, the Gimcracks and the border would be proved out, all three.

The great cat lay on its side, its flanks dilating in the heat. Normally it preferred the higher country where its was cooler and safer. But this was low down in the foothills not far from the ranches where it was hotter and infinitely more dangerous. Where the mottling sunlight touched its coat, filtering down through the tree which shaded it, the fur glinted iridescently, with just the faintest hint of darker jaguar pattern markings showing through the golden brown.

This result of the chance mating between a puma and a wandering Mexican jaguar male drifting far to the north of its accustomed ranges by God knew what wanderlust, hunger or rage, was much larger than any fully grown male mountain lion. Nor did the differences end there. This *La Sombra* was temperamentally much more jaguar than mountain lion, which does not harm man, nor even human women or children. She was a killer of men and the killing rage had never driven her more fiercely than today.

She turned her bullet head in the direction of the high country where buzzards were stripping the bones of her mate bare.

Then she rose with a rumbling rasp in her throat and padded towards the arroyo which snaked away across the desert towards the town. The beast sensed it was reaching the end of its brief journey of power and terror. All that was left now was vengeance.

Smoke trickled from Fidel Trueno's lips as he surveyed the rumpled, sunwashed barricade of the Perro Hills reaching west to east across this raddled landscape south of the border.

'Tell me more, what you hear,' he ordered.

The scout doffed his sombrero. He was a short, fat rider with dark and bulging jowls, which gave him the facial characteristics of a monkey because of an enormously wide mouth like a monkfish. The man was ugly as sin but was the most effective and inexhaustible scout the Majestic Mountain *bandido* had ever known.

Monkey Face had plenty to report. Most significant for Trueno was the revelation of a recent gun battle in the Perros resulting in at least one death. No, he did not know the identity of the dead man although it was rumored to have been an outlaw.

'You mean like us?' Trueno was an outlaw and proud of it. He sprang from a family of outlaws of which he was the sole survivor, his two brothers having lost their lives on a gibbet in Amarillo, Texas two years earlier.

'Gringo outlaw, *caudillo*,' Monkey Face informed him.

That did it for Trueno, who immediately swung down from his black horse and threw his reins at one of his fifteen-man band before drawing the cheroot from his lips.

'You, Juan and Pablo,' he ordered, 'scout the Perros and see if the passes are safe before I go another mile. I come to kill, not to be killed. *Vamamos*! Go!'

Two hours later found the *bandido* trio trotting warily across a rocky plateau 1,000 feet above the plains. They knew the Perros well from various raids conducted in the old days, before Trueno had settled down to rule the rich lands around Diaz City from his eyrie on the mountain. This was bleak and desolate country, largely avoided by honest men, through which wound several rough trails utilized in the past by Mexican and American gangs raiding one another's towns and ranches.

Monkey Face led his men to a look-out spot above the first pass, which proved devoid of life. He was leading them through a series of brushy hollows *en route* to the next trail to the east, when a rifle churned above them and the rider to his right let out a ragged scream, fought to cling to his plunging mount, then crashed head first to the earth with a hole as large as a fist in his back where the soft-nosed .50 bullet had torn through. The second scout almost made it to the cover of a huge and twisted old oak before a volley of shots ripped across his back to smash him over his horses's head, the animal itself going down moments later beneath a brutally excessive leaden storm.

Only Monkey Face escaped, the way he had often made it in the past. Reactive speed of reflex combined with innate horsemanship saw him rake and lift his cayuse into a huge, leaping plunge, carrying him away even before the first ambush victim had crashed from his saddle.

Monkey Face was a survivor, yet despite living through that first deafening barrage, he was still not out of danger yet as horsemen appeared from woods higher up to come racing downslope behind flaming guns.

Gringo horsemen.

Somehow the scout was not surprised by this. Surprise didn't strike until a racing, headlong half-mile further on as he stormed back the way they'd come. A squat American astride a wall-eyed white mare came out of nowhere behind a bucking gun.

Monkey Face dropped low and triggered back to

89

catch the attacker in the lower chest with two brilliant shots which were the last thing the man ever heard.

As he rushed onwards, ducking his big hat below low branches and muttering '*Jesu Cristo!*' over and over, he knew he'd seen that ambusher before; he had fitted a name to the face before he crossed the trickling creek at the toe of the hills.

Jory Hudd rode with Cheeko Rafer. And Rafer and Trueno shared a vicious rivalry which extended back over years.

Trueno received the report with ice-cold fury one hour later.

'Now we understand,' he said savagely. 'By some means Rafer has discovered I intend leaving to travel north. He fears he might not be able to attack me there, so he has schemed to ambush me here on the trails. How fortunate that I was wise enough to send you ahead, Monkey Face, otherwise it could well be me lying dead up there.'

Big hats nodded in full agreement. Better anyone else cash in his chips rather than the great Trueno.

'I do not know how many, Fidel,' the scout panted, still sweating from his furious ride. 'But Rafer is up there in strength.'

Trueno surveyed the dun-colored façade of the Perros as one word trickled from his lips. '*Zopilote!* Buzzard.' It was his long-time pejorative for a man he had always regarded as an inferior. Cheeko Rafer might be obsessed with the ambition to kill him and thus become a badman of stature in his adopted country, but Trueno had always treated the man as nothing. Perhaps he was vaguely impressed by the fact that Rafer had gone to such lengths to learn of his movements, yet he still refused to rate the man as anything more than an annoyance. He would enter the hills and rid himself of Rafer once and for all to leave the way clear for him to accomplish his true mission, a sacred mission of far greater importance than feeding Cheeko Rafer's liver and lights to the coyotes.

'We shall bypass the hills,' he announced. He pointed west with his cheroot. 'The Caramillo Trail.'

'But, Fidel,' protested a black-mustached lieutenant, 'this will take days.'

'One day!' Trueno corrected. 'We shall ride until our horses fall dead beneath us, then we shall walk if needs be. Every breath drawn by the killer I seek now is an insult to the sacred memory of my brothers.'

CHAPTER 6

REVENGE IS SWEET

Restless and uneasy, Buck Dulane walked beneath the shadow of the cottonwoods planted in an uneven row down one side of the street along the central block. Restlessness was part of this man's make-up, yet uneasiness rarely troubled him at quiet times such as this. And Limbo was very quiet that evening despite the upheavals and excitement of the previous day. It was as if the town was a little hungover from hunting and celebrating and getting the pants scared off them by that critter raising a racket up in the hills.

Then again, this could simply be Limbo's instinctive way of getting itself back to the safety and security of the dull and everyday tempo of life it found far more natural and desirable than any other. The planks of the boardwalk had contracted and expanded in the summer heat, and his boot-heels made hard-edged sounds as he walked, looking round for sign of the kid.

Funny thing about that kid. Boy Johnny made him feel good, at times, even filled his head with notions of what it might be like to have children of his own – dangerous stuff like that. Or, leastways, it was dangerous for a man who almost made a religion of keeping moving, avoiding entanglements, sniffing the winds and heading always for the places that smelt of excitement, action, good whiskey and bad women.

That thought held him momentarily as he continued his wandering, trying to decide whether to go or stay another day. He'd known many women, brown and white, fresh-faced country innocents, housemaids and débutantes, shrewd widows, divorcees, oversexed saloon singers and haughty ladies of commerce. He had enjoyed them all, lavished love and money on most, but then sooner or later always found some reason to go.

There was one woman in Limbo who seemed more disturbingly attractive than almost any he'd known, and this was troubling him as he made his way towards the eatery, thumbs hooked in pockets, hat thrust to the very back of his head. Somehow whenever he got to thinking of Jean Kelly, Boy Johnny also sprang to mind. He seemed to connect them in his thinking. Two Limbo denizens who did not seem to deserve Limbo, yet were trapped in it like flies in aspic, one by her loneliness and the other by his childhood.

Dulane had a momentary foolish impulse to invite them to leave with him. To show them there was another side to life before the woman's beauty faded to desert dryness and whatever fate befell kids like Johnny overtook him. Crazy, of course.

The set pattern of his life was to attract trouble, enjoy it, extricate himself from it, get his money and move on. Not concern himself about other folks, who most likely, if only he really knew, might be better suited to their seemingly sad lives than he was to his.

He entered the eatery and glanced at the sign above the counter:

TODAY'S SPECIAL
NO CREDIT

He ordered pork chops with collard greens and coffee to wash it down. The place was half-full and the customers and staff were still talking lions. It was plain they expected him to join in but he made it patently plain that he wasn't interested. Nobody seemed peeved by his rudeness. This was a town where nobody got too carried away by anything, although that hair-curling scream the lion had laid over them last night had succeeded in getting them going for a while.

'Mr Branson wants to get another party together to go up there tomorrow,' he heard the counterman inform a depot hand. 'Says it might be a wounded cat that should be put out of its misery.'

'He can count me out,' said Dundee, the retired peace officer. 'That shrieking thing didn't sound any too sick to me. What it sounded like was good and mad and that ain't the way I like my big game nohow.'

'Well, you know Mr Branson, he loves to hunt,' the counterman said. 'Gets rid of some of that energy of his, I guess.'

'And cussedness,' put in a youth who was eating potatoes. 'Could be one of the hardest and cussedest *hombres* I've ever met behind those fine manners and tailored duds of his.'

The remarks drew no response. Dulane did not expect them to. Branson was an oak standing tall amongst sickly paloverdes here. The man might well be hard, but he provided Limbo with a strong core. Not that Dulane gave much of a damn about that, of course.

His food arrived. He was starting in on it when Henri the Painter said, 'In any case, I reckon Branson might be one of the few who really believes in this *La Sombra* rubbish. But there's no outsized cat up there. It's a puma just like any other, mad or not. Don't you agree, Buck?'

'Nope.'

Everyone stared. The counterman said, 'You sayin' there is, fella?'

'For what it's worth,' Dulane said, reluctant to get involved, 'I rode up there today and saw some tracks.' He paused then added, 'Big, right enough, maybe bigger than I ever saw.' Another pause as the room buzzed about him. 'And he or she is good and mad, like you say, Louis. So I guess it wouldn't be smart for Branson or anyone else to go up there with a gun alone right now.' He almost regretted putting forward his opinion, the way it got them going. But they mainly left him alone to finish his meal in peace, which he appreciated, for he still had some decision-making to do. He paid his money, rolled a cigarette and was about to light it and leave when a couple of urchins entered the eatery, looking concerned.

Turned out they'd been exploring the dry creek-bed north of town with Boy Johnny just on dusk. When they returned to town, Johnny had not come back with them, instead insisting he was 'going hunting'. After supper the boys checked on the pile of crates in back of the general store which Boy Johnny shared with his uncle. Irish, drunk as usual, claimed he'd not seen his nephew since mid afternoon – and now his friends were still searching for him a full hour later.

They found tracks left by the boy's bare feet in the sandy creek bottom by lanternlight well north of where the children had been playing. But there was no sign of Boy Johnny himself.

Eldio the wood carter was nodding over reins and whip as the little cart jarred and jolted its way along something that he might call a trail but which to most others was scarcely a track winding down through the Gimcrack foothills.

It was midnight and hills and desert lay beneath moonlight almost as bright as day, the cart was laden high and Limbo was still ten miles to the south and east.

Eldio rarely travelled this late but he had broken a wheel back in the canyon, which had delayed him over a day. He was weary, overdue at home and so had convinced himself that he should strike out from his camp at sunset instead of waiting for dawn as ordinarily he would have done.

He'd underestimated his weariness and not even the bone-jarring motion of the unsprung cart or the protesting braying of his *burro* could jolt him from his drowsiness for more than a few seconds at a time before he was slipping back into a half-sleep, thinking of his dark-eyed young bride and his friends at the Cobweb Palace, where they would drink wine and roister for the next two or three days before it was time to return to the hills where he made his living.

The wood carter had encountered nobody but an ancient hermit hunting rabbits in several days, and knew nothing of events in the town or anyplace beyond the limits of the woods where he plied his axe.

Coming off the decline, the equipage trundled along a wide, moon-flooded gullywash where sickly trees hung over red sand and an owl hooted once from a thicket.

With easier going beneath his wheels, Eldio was slumping lower in his seat and beginning to snore a little when the rig came to a sudden halt, throwing him against the splashboard and jarring him awake.

'*Zopilote!*' he protested to the *burro*, which was standing with long ears both pointed skywards. 'Buzzard! *Idiota!* Why do you halt, foolish one?'

He thrust his hat back from his head with a powerful arm and gazed round at flooding moonlight and black shadow, thinking how quiet it was, then cursing himself for so thinking.

'It is the middle of the night. What do you expect? Miss Jean's dancer and her tambourine?' He took a fresh grip of his reins, promised himself to stay awake, slapped the *burro*'s hindquarters. 'Proceed, *estúpido*.'

Instead the *burro* began backing into the shafts, tail tucked under, ears quivering. Eldio emitted another curse and was reaching for the whip when he also caught the scent. Instantly goosebumps appeared along his brown forearms, for it was a smell any outdoorsman in this sector of the country would identify immediately. Feral, musky and sharp.

Mountain lion!

It was true that no genuine outdoorsman feared the shy puma. But the very fact that the animal scent was so strong just here was enough to alarm tough and muscular Eldio, and saw him reaching for his rusty old rifle as his gaze panned around the wash. Surely the creature must be close. Yet why had it not fled at his approach? It could be dead, of course, although the *burro*'s terrified reaction suggested otherwise. It was perfectly all right for a stupid *burro* to be afraid. Unlike man, *burros* were not excluded from a hungry puma's diet.

The man jumped down. No point in trying to flog the *burro* on; it wouldn't budge. He felt peeved and only vaguely uneasy as he he moved about, shouting to scare the critter away.

Suddenly the beast was there directly before him, standing motionless in the red sand. Eldio blinked and breathed, '*Nombre de Dios*!' The lion was larger than any he had ever seen, the impact of its presence exaggerated further by the silent abruptness of its appearance and the fact that it was not acting the way he'd seen any big cat do in the presence of man.

It was almost the size of the jaguars he had hunted as a young man down in Ocotillo Province. Yet size was not the most alarming thing about this cat. It was the intensity of its stare that chilled him. Suppressed rage? Total hatred? Whatever it was it burned in the animal's opaque yellow eyes, raised the fur along its spine, invested its movements with a terrible grace.

It was coming forward!

Eldio whipped up his rifle and triggered once before the leaping beast struck him and tore out his throat. It was over in a moment, but that was sufficient time for the *burro* to hurl itself against the harness straps and take off along the wash at a terrified gallop, scattering bundles of wood as the cart bounced and bucked behind.

The killer followed at a heavy, muscular trot, but not trying to overtake. It just happened that it had been following the same trail as Eldio when they met in the wash. The trail to Limbo.

Midday and still no news.

Jean Kelly stepped out onto the saloon porch for perhaps the dozenth time that morning to shield her eyes with one hand and stare off along Fort Street to the north. She called a question to a waddy riding by but the man just shrugged and spread his hands. No, he had heard no news on Dulane's search for Boy Johnny either. Then as he passed on by, he turned in

99

the saddle and called, 'Wouldn't fuss too much if I was you, Miz Jean. He's always on the wander, that one. He'll show. Likely just hidin' to get folks all stirred up. Or most likely dodgin' Irish, heh, heh.'

'Your ass!' she muttered, in a most unladylike way, then clapped a hand to her mouth. The penalty of working in a saloon, she thought. You picked up the drinkers' bad habits.

Then: 'How could they be looking so long without finding him? Where on earth are they searching. . . ?'

She did not hear the rider coming. She glanced casually at him as she made for the doors, then paused to take a second look when he nodded to her in a familiar way as though he knew her, doffing his hat with the hint of a smile.

'Miss Jean.' His voice was young as his face. He appeared to be around seventeen, slim, straight, fair-complexioned – and curiously other-worldly, she imagined. 'Name's Danny. But I guess that wouldn't mean anything to you, huh?'

She didn't know him but felt she should. 'How do you do . . . Danny?'

'Well, not too well if you must know the truth, Miss Jean,' he revealed, swinging to earth more lightly than any horseman she'd ever seen. Sky-blue eyes scanned the street. 'Seems to me there shouldn't be nigh so many able-bodied *hombres* still down here on the street when that boy is still missing.' She moved to the edge of the porch.

'You've heard about little Johnny then?'

'Surely.' He mounted the steps and she found it difficult to take her eyes from his face. There was something undoubtedly strange yet appealing about this slim and fair-headed youth. 'Always bad when a kid goes missing, ma'am. Especially when there's a river about. Yes, ma'am, a big old river like the Majestic can reach out and gobble up a little tad of a kid like . . .'

His voice cut off abruptly. He shook his fair head with a frown then looked at her with eyes as level as gunbarrels.

'Do you have any notion why these customers of yours are sitting about drinking liquor when they should be out there with Buck Dulane?'

She was offended by the implied accusation, but didn't let it show. He interested her; she wasn't sure why.

'Oh, you know Mr Dulane also?'

'Good man. And they are good men with him. Only thing, there aren't enough of them. This is a big country, dangerous too.'

Jean turned away to move slowly to the end of the gallery, feeling the heat of the breeze coming in off the desert against her face. Habitually schooling herself against emotion, which she did as naturally as breathing, she felt weakened and somehow betrayed by the emotion she was feeling now. The child missing, Dulane gone after him, both swallowed by this 'big dangerous' land; she had never felt more helpless nor so strangely vulnerable.

When she looked again, the young rider had vanished inside. In the middle distance, the familiar figure of a walking man caused her to start in astonishment.

She had naturally expected Branson to be still out with Dulane's small handful of searchers!

Branson was removing his hat as he reached the saloon, affronting her even further with his familiar fat smile.

'Mr Branson! What on earth are you doing here?'

He appeared puzzled as he joined her by the batwings. 'I don't understand, Miss Jean . . .'

'Why aren't you . . . out there?'

'Oh, all the commotion about the child, you mean? Well, my dear, it's not the first time some young shaver has gone off and misplaced his way in the chaparral, I'm sure. In any case, there are enough men out there to—'

'He's not just any child, Mr Ethan Branson. And in case I have to remind you, there are dangerous animals out there. I . . . I thought you would have been the first to saddle up!'

'For God's sake, woman, it's only a ragged urchin, and a none too polite one, if I may add.'

Jean swung away and vanished through the doors, flinging them aside as she came through, causing heads to turn. She was behind her bar, dabbing at her eyes when a bemused Branson entered. The man was angry. Nobody ever stood in judgment of Ethan Branson; it was unheard of.

'Jean, I demand an apology,' he said loudly, seemingly unaware of anyone else but her as he came striding to the bar. 'You have no right condemning me in that way. I always do my duty as you well know. The child has run off somewhere, probably from that drunken lout of an uncle of his, and that is surely no reason for the entire town to turn itself on its ear.'

'Who . . . who's a drunken lout?'

Branson whirled to see the weaving, red-faced figure of Irish O'Neil lurch from an alcove in back. O'Neil's way of showing his concern at the child's disappearance was not to go searching but rather to drink so much as to render him incapable of doing anything other than drinking some more.

'Who said that?' the man demanded, then slewed to a halt as he came face to face with Branson. 'Oh, Mr Branson sir. How do you do, your grace.'

'Isn't it wonderful?' Jean's sarcastic voice carried to every corner. 'A little boy goes missing, his uncle gets drunk, our most enthusiastic hunter and civic father fails to lift a finger to help, and a dozen able-bodied men sit around drinking and talking when they could every one of them be out helping Doc and Mr Dulane. You know, I've never felt ashamed of this town until today.'

Even Branson seemed to falter a little before this tirade, while O'Neil burst into guilty tears and the drinkers dropped their eyes to their glasses. But whether or not Jean's words would have any lasting effect was uncertain as a full minute passed without further reaction, until the slender young stranger stepped forward.

'Miss Jean's so right, pards,' he said in that winning way he seemed to have. 'The kid needs all the help he can get right now, or you could lose him. Nothing's worth losing a kid. But heck, you all know that well as I do. Only thing Miss Jean's wrong about, she doesn't know you've just been waiting for the right moment to grab your hats, saddle your broncs and ride out with me to join the search-parties. Well, now's the right time and we're all just itching for some action. Isn't that right, Irish?'

'Huh? Oh, why ... er, guess it is,' muttered a puzzled O'Neil.

'And just who the hell are you, kid?' demanded a voice from the crowd.

'Danny, of course, Ringo,' the young rider replied, spreading his hands and smiling. 'You all know me, boys.'

Funny thing was, it almost felt as if they did, he was that likeable, friendly and somehow vaguely familiar, or so they felt. And he certainly seemed to know all of them. He even winked companionably at Branson as he moved towards the batwings as though anticipating that he would follow.

'Just a minute—' Branson began harshly, but Jean's voice cut him off.

'Go with him, Mr Branson,' she said sharply. 'And you too, Irish O'Neil. And the rest of you. And don't come back until you find Johnny. And if you don't find him I'll hold each one of you personally responsible.'

'Well, you heard the lady,' Danny said, holding the batwings open. 'I heard tell they're looking out by the Segura fault right now. Who wants to be last man to get there, huh?'

Nobody seemed to quite understand what was happening; they were aware of a compulsion to follow this personable young rider in a way that was strange and powerful. But fear maintained its icy grip

104

over most, and eventually only a shame-faced O'Neil and one other drunk trailed Danny out.

It was hard for Branson to knuckle under, being the kind of man he was. But Jean Kelly's stare remained implacable, and soon he too was gone, leaving Jean to whistle up all her will power to refrain from reaching for the bottle with a shaking hand.

That little boy meant more to her than she had realized. And not only him.

CHAPTER 7

QUARRY

He walked on with the brush scratching at his bare legs, hoping he would see the town over the next low rise. But he didn't. Nothing there but more sand and rocks and brush . . . and still no sign of water.

Boy Johnny squatted down in the sparse shade of a brush clump. The hills rippled in the heat and insects droned. It was so still and hushed. In the far distance he glimpsed antelope moving against a yellow dune. Even further out, so far that rising heat waves made everything wavery, there were strange cloud formations that were at once red and orange and the color of dust. High overhead, a couple of eagles wheeled slowly on widespread wings, screaming at regular intervals, their calls quickly sucked up by the huge silence.

A single tear trickled down his cheek. He shut his eyes, hoping that when he opened them again he would find himself back in his packing-crate with

Unc bawling at him for something. But all that had changed was that the eagles had gone planing off towards the Gimcracks, soon to be lost from sight.

He shivered involuntarily as he rose to his feet again. He must steer away from the hills where the lions were. He moved off slowly from sand onto stone where his feet left no mark.

At least, he reassured himself, he still had his gun.

'Danny, huh? Know somehing about tracking and suchlike, do you, Danny?'

'Some, Buck. I take it you're working blind here just at the moment?'

Dulane nodded grimly, watching as the three reluctant new arrivals from town swung down to join his small group of tired searchers.

'We followed his prints about a mile through the washes, then lost them at the rocks by the butte yonder. We've been circling ever since without any luck. But having more hands is sure going to help. I've got to say I'm surprised at Branson and O'Neil showing up. How come?'

Danny shrugged.

'Who knows? Conscience maybe.' Then his unlined face took on a harder look. 'But you know something? I've no time for any man who won't help a kid. Could be I look on that as the lowest crime in the book.'

Dulane was interested enough to submit the young rider to a longer second look. He found Danny an interesting yet somewhat strange addition to the still small group. He had no notion where the slender youth had come from, while curiously nobody else seemed really aware of the man's presence, or at least gave that impression.

Danny met his curious stare and for some reason the man of the gun felt a kind of tingling in his wrists, until he glanced away.

You must be letting this caper get to you, Dulane, an inner voice said. *Not like you, boyo. Maybe you're getting a mite old for these kind of capers?* 'The hell I am!' he grunted aloud, then turned to study the rest of the talent on offer. They looked OK, and he was ready and eager to make use of any fresh manpower, which he proceeded to do. In the absence of anybody else showing an inclination to take charge he would continue to lead from up front as he had from the outset.

He proceeded to break the party up into pairs and designated certain specific areas to be searched. They were in the Mesquite Flats region, some five miles across, which reached from the malapai and Sentinel Butte east-west line, to the foothills northwest and the desert proper northeast.

Morale and enthusiasm were running low despite the addition of three new 'volunteers'. Several had brought liquor along, including the missing boy's uncle who'd naturally had to borrow a horse.

Before dispatching his two-man parties, Dulane gathered them together to deliver a tough enough address. He welcomed the presence of the new men and knew they were as concerned for the child's safety as himself, he assured them all. But just in case they might be considering merely going through the motions today before finding excuses to return to town as soon as possible – they could forget that. They would be returning to Limbo when they had Boy Johnny with them, safe and sound, not before. All of them. This said, they were now free to get mounted and begin searching.

As they moved off, he turned to find that Ethan Branson had come up behind to listen.

'Amazing what a little authority will do to some men, Mr Dulane. There was no need to talk to those fellows that way.'

'Want to take over?'

'Why, no, I—'

'Then get on that flash horse of yours and go join Doc at the draw!'

Branson turned pale and tight-lipped. 'All this uproar about one urchin! But of course I understand your real motivation, mister. It's so obvious it's pathetic.'

'It is?'

'Certainly. You understand Miss Jean's attachment to the child and see an opportunity to enhance your standing in her eyes.'

'Guess you're a real good judge of character, eh, Branson?'

'There is none better,' Branson shot back, tall and commanding. 'I see through men, analyse their motives, have developed total insight into good and evil, strength and weakness. You are of a type known to me. You play to the gallery with no real substance to support you. Your flashy appeal attracts a certain kind of woman and you always let them down. In short, I find you quite transparent and disagreeable, sir, and I'd like to take this opportunity to warn you to keep away from Miss Jean when and if we return safely from this foolishness.'

Dulane opened his mouth to respond. Then he saw the young man Danny sitting his horse, waiting impatiently for him, his frown reminding him what they were doing.

He turned without a word, took his horse from a cowboy, stepped up and rode off. Branson glared after his receding figure for a moment, then found his eye drawn to the slim, denim-garbed rider at his side. He rubbed his powerful jaw and his frown cut deep. Dulane, he was quite sure, understood only too clearly. He wished he could be as clear about this Danny drifter. He resented the newcomer's involvement and the way he seemed to be able to influence people, yet could not seem actually to dislike him any more than he wanted actually to go against him.

This was a strange situation for Ethan Branson to find himself in, for he really did know and understand men far better than most. Which, of course, was not the same thing as saying he found mankind in general either admirable or likeable. On the contrary. Hate was one of two prime emotions that drove the man Limbo knew as Ethan Branson, and both were the indirect reasons why such an accomplished and cultivated man had buried himself someplace just about as far from civilization as a man could get.

Doc Belden called to him across the shimmering sand. He mounted up and rode off to rejoin the hunt.

110

*

Her father used to say: 'Things are never so bad they can't get a whole lot worse, little Jeanie.'

But she had never subscribed to that pessimistic view, not even when her life had taken sad turnings, driving her to the life she led now. She still tried to be positive even if she doubted she would ever be happy again, yet had to concede that the events of the past twenty-four hours had succeeded in just about using up all the optimism she could muster.

Miss Jean had never realized just how important a little street-urchin had become to her until he wasn't there any longer. But she had a counter-measure whenever things threatened to get too much for her and late afternoon found her heading for the O.K. Feed Stables to avail herself of it yet again.

She'd acquired her good horse and rubber-tired buggy the same time as she'd bought the saloon. She never used it for business, only for pleasure and relaxation. Two or three afternoons a week she was to be seen driving around town or out along the trails, a serious but smartly tailored figure seated erect on her cushions, usually with the top back. Miss Jean always drove alone.

Today's drive helped some but did not ease her tensions. She knew that that was an impossible expectation. At one point she reined the horse in on a rise along the Overland Mail trail to stare northward in the late afternoon light, imagining what was taking place out there, praying that already there was a messenger galloping towards Limbo with the news that the search had been successful.

Her way back led along the river, now running very low and brown at this time of year. She first slowed then reined in upon sighting a familiar figure walking along the north bank not far from the bridge.

'Good evening, madame!' she called.

Madame Caspar seemed lost in thought, but turned when Jean called again. 'Oh, good evening, Miss Jean. Tell me, have they found him?'

She knew madame would be concerned, having lost her own child under tragic circumstances long ago.

'Not yet, but they shall,' she called back.

The woman held up a rosary. 'I pray for the little one . . . and for my own.' Jean bit her lower lip as she drove on, the rubber tires moving silently over the smooth ground. There was so much sadness in life, she thought. Surely happiness was the hardest thing of all to find.

The sudden stutter of hoofbeats on the bridge startled her and caused her horse to shy. She reined in, eyes widening as half a dozen wild-looking horsemen went sweeping by, coming in off the border trail on travel-stained mounts, rifle butts, spurs and sixgun handles reflecting the slowly fading light.

The party loped right on by, scattering gravel as they swung into Chisum Street before vanishing behind the general store.

Jean's heart lifted to her throat.

As mistress of the Cobweb Palace she encountered virtually everyone who passed through town. Losers were plentiful out here but genuine badmen were a rarity. There was nothing here to attract them. Yet she could still identify that breed on sight, and these were surely the real thing. A gang of hellions descending on Limbo right now – of all times!

Seemed like her father had been right after all.

Although not fully aware of it yet, this incident for Jean Kelly was the last straw. Her restlessness and dissatisfaction with her life here had been growing for some time, and then the arrival of a certain stranger followed by the disappearance of Boy Johnny had succeeded in arousing formerly suppressed emotions that she was no longer sure she could deal with.

First thing in the morning she would call on the realtor who had been making generous offers to buy the Cobweb Palace from her all year. She had packed up and moved on with her life before; she could do it again. But, of course, only after they found the boy.

They were tired men at sundown.

Horses' heads drooped and boots dragged in hot sand as the searchers led their heavy-legged mounts across yet another shallow saucer of Mesquite Flats, an inhospitable region they now knew more intimately than any of them had ever wished to.

They squinted their eyes against the sunset glare but could no longer see Dulane and the young stranger up ahead, where a series of thorny thickets led on to the next stretch of waste.

Suddenly a pistol shot shattered the hush; the signal that something had been found.

In mere moments they were in their saddles and

booting protesting horses over the barricade to bring Dulane and Danny eventually into sight. The pair had stumbled upon the boy's footprints leading out from a section of slab-rock country and heading for a shallow canyon marked by half a dozen live oaks about a half-mile ahead.

Spirits immediately lifted and men were swigging from their canteens and talking animatedly amongst themselves again as they rapidly closed in on the canyon while the red sun plummeted behind the horizon.

In the canyon mouth they found Boy Johnny's prints again, yet these were no longer as clearly defined as they'd been before.

Overlaying them now were the heavy pug-marks of a big cat.

Buck Dulane sat down heavily upon a rock and smoked, listening to nightwind brush over rocks and sand and the murmuring, protesting voices of the townsmen as they sprawled on the uneven ground below him. The hunters were exhausted and so was he. Only difference was he would be still forging on had they been willing to keep up. And, of course, had he known which way he should go. The sign was lost, had been for hours. The tracks of the child and the monster stalking him beneath this brute of a moon had last been seen two miles back before they faded in stony ground.

They'd scouted, quartered, run themselves ragged under his insistent commands. Now they slumped exhausted, in the back of each man's mind the dread

114

that the next sound they heard might be a child's cry of terror or a triumphant scream as chilling and awesome as the primitive howl they'd heard the night of the dance.

He sucked from his canteen and let his eyes play over hummock, dune, rock-formation and stunted tree. His cheeks were stubbled and he appeared to have aged a decade in just a couple of days. Not for a moment had he questioned his involvement here, for beneath his brash exterior he had always been the kind of man to respond spontaneously in a crisis. Of course it peeved him that the majority of his small party seemed to feel they were doing something exceptional and marvellous, putting themselves through all this for Irish O'Neil's ragged kid.

Yet no one had yet quit the hunt. They didn't dare. He'd use Colts to stop them if he must.

He lowered his head, smoke trickling from his lips. He knew he had it in him to hunt the night through without them, all next day and then the following night again. But he simply did not know where to begin to look now. Nobody did. Whether aware that death was stalking him or not, little Johnny had taken an unpredictable turning somewhere and could now be at any one of the 360 points of the compass from this chunk of ancient lava upon which he was seated.

'Hey, Dulane!' someone called. 'Yonder he comes!'

He jerked to his feet to see the indistinct outline of rider and horse appearing on the crest of a moonsilvered ridge at distance to the northwest. He swore under his breath. He'd been riled with Danny for simply disappearing without a word earlier, was now irrationally disappointed to see the man returning without a small figure perched before him upon his saddle cantle. 'Only ever rely on yourself, Dulane,' he muttered bitterly, repeating one of the axioms he lived by.

Only then did he realize that Buck Dulane, the self-sufficient man of the wild and lonely places, had allowed himself to become dependent on a strange slip of a youth he barely knew in a way he'd rarely done with men he'd known all his life.

Doc Belden appeared at his side, a frail wisp of a man who seldom got peeved about anything.

'What do you make of him, Buck?' he wanted to know.

'What the hell do you mean ?' He was brusque. Couldn't help it. He was wearing thin. This was one failure he couldn't accept.

'Your pal. The kid. Don't you think there's something real strange about this Danny?'

'Like what?' He'd been too absorbed in the search to notice much of anything else.

'Did you notice he doesn't drink? At all? Nothing?'

'Bullshit! Course he does. Anyway, he—'

'He's a kid who speaks like a wise old man. He doesn't get tired and he seems to know exactly what he's doing when even you seem to be getting a little jambaxed and strained. And where did he hail from anyway? You must admit it makes you think, Buck.'

'It makes me think maybe you've had too much sun – that's what it makes me think.' He strode away, waving. 'Hey, boy, find anything?'

'Got a big hunch we should check out Smoky Bluff yonder, Buck,' came Danny's cheerful response, which immediately raised a chorus of protesting groans from the dark figures scattered across the rocky depression.

'You got a lead?' Buck demanded.

'Just a hunch.'

Buck raised his eyes to the hills. They were stalled at the toe of the Gimcracks on the ruggedly inaccessible southeastern corner where a series of bluffs buttressed the rearing slopes. Smoky Bluff brooded down upon them, as forbidding as a fortress.

'These men barely made it this far,' he snapped as Danny reined in before him. 'There's no way they could start climbing right now.'

'Likely not. But you and I can. I'm limber, and you're pig-headed. Just bring your rifle, Buck.'

'Don't tell me what to do.'

'We're wasting time.'

'And where is your canteen?'

'Around.'

Dulane stared. 'And you're not wearing a gun!' he accused.

The young man was unruffled. 'Don't need one.'

'But damnit, I . . .'

Danny turned his horse. 'It's a good strong hunch I got about the bluff and I came back to share it with you, Buck. But if you're not interested, I'll go check it out myself,' he stated, and started off.

Dulane was scowling darkly after him when Doc Belden spoke quietly in back. 'I'd go with him if I

117

were you, Buck.'

He rounded on the little medico. 'Whose side are you on anyway, damnit? You put those notions into my head about him in the first place.'

The doc spread his hands.

'I just said he was strange, is all. I didn't say he doesn't seem to know what he's talking about. Better hasten, man or he'll get away on you.'

With a curse, Dulane ran to his horse. He was forced to remind himself that Danny hadn't made a single wrong call since dragging several reluctant searchers out of town to join them at Mesquite Flats. It made sense to keep betting on a lucky dice-roller until he crapped out. He didn't see too many alternatives this moon-stricken night.

CHAPTER 8

SAVAGE HATE

Moonlight flooded the dramatic landscape as the travel-streaked horsemen rode up from the south. From far out along the desert fringe came the lonesome howling of a single coyote rebuking the moon for its finding itself all alone on so romantic a night.

And as soon as the dark riders and laboring horses had worked their way clear of thornbrush and cactus they could see the silvery trace of the Majestic River and the dim lights of the town straddling the Wells Fargo trail.

Trueno's raised right hand brought the party to an immediate halt. The dust-coated face of the leader of the pack was taut with suspicion as he thrust back his hat. He had set a ferocious pace coming up by the roundabout Caramillo Trail, but now that their objective lay in clear sight before them he seemed lassoed by suspicion.

'All their lights on at this time of the night?' he

119

hissed. 'What could be the reason for this?'

No response. From Monkey Face to scar-featured Rivera, the rebel-*bandidos* were as puzzled as he. Yet it did not take long for the leader to sniff about and pick up a suspicious scent.

'Rafer!' he said hollowly yet with certainty. 'We puzzled why that maggot-eater did not return to attack us again in the hills in the wake of our clash. Now it is plain. Rather than risk losing more men in the Perros he obviously chose to come on ahead with the intent of ambushing us here at the town.'

Exhausted and hollow-eyed long-riders traded weary looks. They were reluctant to contest what sounded to them like pure speculation, for the good reason that their leader's instincts usually proved more reliable than other men's nailed-down hard facts.

Even so, Monkey Face felt moved to pose the obvious query.

'But, *caudillo*, how could the evil Cheeko know we were riding here to Limbo?'

'The same way as he knows about the Judge!'

'The Judge' was never a name to be mentioned lightly in this company. Indeed it had been a name constantly evoked by Trueno for two years, ever since his last visit to *Los Estados Unidos* where his life had been blighted by loss as savage and cruel as any he himself had inflicted upon the lives of so many others.

In the two years since the days his brothers had been hanged the butcher of Musketoon Mountain had concentrated on consolidating his criminal stranglehold over the Diaz City region from his mountain stronghold, while at the same time organizing and financing search after search for the former so-called Hanging Judge Ira Black of Amarillo.

It had taken all of that two years to achieve success, but merely a few short days for Trueno to complete his preparations then set out on his holy mission of vengeance for the judge's hiding-place, namely this strangely illuminated lonesome town crouching amongst its giant trees on the riverland before him now.

'We still do not understand how Rafer could know about the judge being in Limbo, Fidel,' a black-bearded throat-slitter remarked.

'That *zopilote* found out because I realized almost too late that this would-be *bandido* king has almost forgotten how to plunder and kill and steal. Instead he has been so obsessed with jealousy of my power he has been using all his resources to spy upon my movements and thus had in the end, come to uncover my plans. I understood all this when I realized that he had set up the ambush for me in the Perros . . . the attack which failed against that gringo *pistolero*, Dulane.'

He paused to set fire to a thin black cigarillo. The forced ride from the Perros had been brutal but Trueno still managed to radiate a steely stamina. 'When I declared I would seek out Judge Black and destroy him one day, the evil judge believed me and vanished from sight in sheer terror. Rafer also believed me because he knew I would do as I said, avenge myself on Black. We knew at the time that

that gun dog was keeping watch on my Black-hunters. I believe now, that when they were eventually able to inform me of Black's hiding-place, Rafer's agents were there to buy this information from them For two years the evil Cheeko has been waiting to catch me far from my stronghold and kill me, and suddenly he sees his chance. He realized I would come after Black and that nothing would stop me.'

The *bandidos* nodded understandingly. This certainly sounded like the rebels' most dangerous enemy right enough.

'But what kind of *idiota* is Rafer if he believes that to simply draw you away from Musketoon Mountain should bring him success?' a man beneath a huge hat puzzled. 'We see him only as a lowly carrion-eater who feeds on the remains of others. What makes this gringo think he could conquer the mighty Trueno?' This might sound unctuous to the untrained ear. But the truth of it was that Trueno had so inculcated his henchmen with the notion that Cheeko Rafer was nothing more than an envy-ridden incompetent, that they believed it now.

'Rafer has shown time and time again he will go to any lengths to destroy me in the dream of taking over my empire and reputation – the son of a bitch dog!'

Trueno paused to tug at a golden earring and to calm his lethal furies.

'But now, seeing this town alive with light in the dead heart of the night fills me with the gravest alarm. What smarter thing for Rafer to do than withdraw from ambush into the hills, then ride ahead to await for me here, where he knows I must come sooner or later after Judge Black? It is what I myself would do in such a position. He is a fool without *cojones*, but even such a one might have brains enough to make such a plan.'

It still seemed to some that their leader might be drawing too long a bow in jumping from what was known to what was merely assumed.

One man ventured the counter-theory that citizens might simply be staging an all-night fiesta in Limbo, such as they sometimes did in Diaz City. Another's conjecture was that perhaps the Wells Fargo coaches could well be in the habit of changing teams here in the wee small hours. Who could be sure what the strange gringos might do in a cemetery town such as this? Yet no one openly challenged the leader's theory. He hated his underlings disagreeing with him, and it could prove a highly dangerous practice.

But Monkey Face did have a query: 'Fidel, *mi compañero*, if it is the Cheeko, and if he awaits us here with his gang as you think, surely it would be wise for us to be cautious about rushing straight in to seek out the Hanging Judge?'

The *bandido* chief slowly shook his head. Were it simply a case of Fidel Trueno versus Cheeko Rafer up here in dangerous gringo country, he might well have elected to withdraw and fight another day. But it had taken two long years of a festering hatred, endured to track Black to his den, and Trueno had not enjoyed one untroubled night's sleep since the judge had hanged his beloved, backshooting brothers.

'Each of us is worth a dozen gringo dry-gulchers – and Judge Black has lived far too long already,' he snarled. '*Andale*! We ride!'

And they did, swift horses carrying them flowing across the glittering desert, rushing forward to their appointment with destiny while Trueno's darkest memories carried him back into the past. . . .

The stage was set and Death lurked in the wings.

The square and surrounding streets of Amarillo were densely packed with excited, blood-hungry Texans, all chanting and shaking clenched fists at the condemned, then howling in adulation as the tall, black-robed figure of the man responsible for this spectacular of justice appeared on the balcony of the Justice Hall to witness the execution of his sentence.

Upon the rickety gallows, two youthful Mexicans in manacles, a portly priest with Book and robes, the dreaded hangman with his face masked from the world, the court official in the blood-red tunic bellowing out the crimes of which the condemned had been found guilty, frequently forced to pause until the deafening chorus of 'Hang them!' faded a little, enabling him to be heard. And disguised, jostled, disbelieving and helpless amongst all the sweating and bellowing of this breed of aliens, the infamous *bandido*, the rebel legend from the south, Fidel Trueno – the real reason why the judge was hanging his brothers.

The two youths had demanded to accompany their outlaw brother when Chivo announced his plans to make a 1000-mile ride to plunder the Texas Express Office in Amarillo, and in the end he had been forced to capitulate. It was to be his first robbery in Texas and his first anywhere with the brothers he had always so jealously protected. How could anything be more fitting? Not just Trueno the bandit king any longer, but The Truenos!

Estupendo!

They found the Rangers waiting for them.

Somehow their plans had leaked out and their capture, incarceration, trial, conviction and life sentences imposed on all three took but one head-line-grabbing day in the life of Amarillo.

But no prison could hold Fidel Trueno, which he quickly proved within forty-eight hours after accomplices smuggled him what was needed to pick a prison lock, slit two gringo throats and vanish over a high wall.

He was feverishly planning the freeing of his brothers when the judge ordered a retrial of Manuel and Miguel Trueno, following which he sentenced each to death by hanging.

Trial, conviction and sentencing had taken place that very morning. A distraught Trueno was 'lucky' to get there just in time to see the trap-doors drop away beneath the boots of his murderous brothers.

This was the judge's long-planned revenge against Trueno, and a splendidly successful revenge it proved to be.

For a month the *bandido* was in hiding, nursing his grief alone. Then he came within a whisper of driving a bullet through the judge's head from ambush during a dinner for dignitaries at the same court house in which his brothers had been sentenced to death.

All Texas appeared to be out hunting Trueno but he was no longer there. He merely delayed his flight long enough to have printed and posted a solemn and sacred vow to take Judge Black's life in repayment for the lives he had stolen from him, and then was gone. The next thing heard of him was that he was back in Sonora plundering, kidnapping and killing just as he'd always done. Trueno never knew how many Texans took his threat of revenge seriously. One who did was the hanging judge himself. Ira Black promptly resigned his commission and literally vanished in that same month and remained that way until a relentless two-year search by his most dangerous enemy eventually pointed a finger at Limbo, Arizona.

Vivid memories slowly merged with tendrils of the past, then slowly began to fade as Trueno realized that the horsemen had come to a halt in the black moon-shadow of a bare hill which stood within rifle shot of the lazy river. Travel-weary *bandidos* stared down at the lit-up town, then back at their *caudillo*. It took some time for Trueno fully to overcome the raging emotions that were invariably aroused whenever he saw in his mind's eye images of two slim figures jerking their lives away at the ends of yellow ropes, while all Texas, it seemed, roared its anathema.

'That ruined adobe farmhouse,' he said at last, hoarsely, gesturing at a long-abandoned cornfield. 'We shall rest there quietly while Rivera inspects this ugly village and reports back on whether I am right or wrong.'

Sunken-eyed Rivera nodded. Pale-skinned and husky, the killer should pass virtually unnoticed in Limbo.

The man swung astride and departed immediately, leaving his *compañeros* to rest. All but the *caudillo*, of course. Sucking an unlighted Cuban, Trueno continued to study the town unblinkingly from an unglazed window, too near to his moment of revenge and too murderously excited to rest his eyes even for a moment.

The terror was close and the child knew it. His heart clenched tight and painful in his chest as he clutched his gun and attempted to squeeze even deeper into the fissure. Johnny's knees and elbows were skinned from his Herculean climb up the flank of the bluff, an ascent motivated by his terror of the monster.

He understood in his childish way that he would be dead by now had he not chanced to sight the panther sniffing at his tracks several hundred yards behind, just as he'd approached the bluffs. Miss Jean had taught him about his guardian angel and he believed it was he who had caused him to look back and see the puma before it sighted him, giving him time to climb.

For perhaps half an hour after making the ascent he'd hoped and prayed that his escape might prove successful; that the killer might lose his scent and simply wander off in search of easier prey.

Then the scent struck him like a blow – pungent, sharp, indescribably savage and frightening.

He heard nothing and saw nothing yet knew that

La Sombra was close. Somehow he squeezed into the fissure which proved barely wide enough to accommodate his small body. He was yet to see the terror up close as he held the gun before him in trembling hands.

Time passed . . . it seemed an eternity.

Then . . .

The flooding moonlight seemed to shiver in the child's vision, and suddenly it was there in that all-revealing light, the great grandmother of all lions padding directly towards his hideaway in that low, slope-shouldered glide that hunting cats have, and the boy no longer knew whether he had a heart or whether it had burst in terror.

The killer thrust its great head inside the fissure, fixing him with its terrible stare. Boy Johnny could see the teeth now, the long curved and wetly gleaming canines and the sharp-ridged molars behind. Sensitive whiskers were drawn back to avoid contact with the fissure walls. Johnny could feel the warmth of feral breath, saw the scars of old battles etched upon yellow hide, sensed what it was like to be in the presence of an almost other-world being as it opened its jaws and emitted a silent snarl.

He screamed as the claw snaked in after him, jabbed at it with the wooden gun. Then the puma emitted its full killing roar and the child could hear nothing above that insane clamor as he wriggled and squeezed his way further back, and the claws and the demon's savage head followed.

The nightmare might have endured for seconds or an hour. There was no telling. Johnny had no concept of time, only of blind terror as he clung desperately to his small life – until he thought his gun went off.

He forced himself to open terror clenched eyes. His gun was still the same old wooden one, carved from a fence-slat. Yet he was certain he had heard the shot – and where was *La Sombra* now?

The lion was nowhere in sight as he thrust his way back along the fissure to catch a glimpse of a scene that etched itself into his mind. There was the lion with its back to him, rearing to its full height on hindlegs and ripping savagely at the air with extended claws. Barely visible beyond the stricken animal, a crouched Buck Dulane was working the lever of his smoking Winchester as he hammered shot after shot into the rearing body until at last the screaming ceased and the big cat crashed to the ground. It came rolling dustily down the incline almost to the feet of a slim young man in blue jeans and shirt who seemed to have appeared from nowhere.

The next moments passed in a blur as Johnny felt himself being dragged out of the shadows into the moonlight, then he was hugged in a way he could not remember, and cried because he didn't know what else to do.

Buck boosted him up onto his shoulder and walked past the cat, which seemed even longer and larger in death. Buck was laughing out loud with relief now, while the young stranger just stood there with one boot up on a rock, smiling at them both.

'This is the man who really saved you, boy,' Dulane insisted. 'He figured where you might be and brought me here. This here is Danny.'

'I knew you'd come, Buck,' Johnny cried. He paused a moment, than added, 'You too, Danny.'

'Now how could you know that, shaver?' Dulane grinned indulgently. 'You don't even know this man.'

'I know,' Johnny said gravely, meeting the blue eyes. 'But I still knew you would come . . . Danny.' He shook his curls, looking a little confused now. 'But how would I know that?'

'Nobody knows all the answers, Boy Johnny,' Danny said in his easy way. 'Not even Buck here, who thinks he knows just about everything. Eh, Buck?'

'That's me, Know-all Buck.' Dulane laughed, giving the boy a tickle. 'Come on, we've got distance to cover. We've got a party to pick up, and there's a certain lady in town who'll skin me with a blunt knife if I'm two seconds late getting you back to see her. Let's go.'

They headed down with Danny leading the way. Although triumphant and happy, Dulane remained vaguely puzzled about why any man would go lion-hunting without a gun.

Irish O'Neil stumbled and fell, almost rolling into the camp-fire. One man laughed wearily but others showed disgust, most notably Ethan Branson for whom this whole enterprise was proving a trial.

'Where the devil does he get liquor out here?' he demanded querulously as someone helped the drunk to his feet.

'You have to know Irish, Ethan,' supplied little Doc

Belden, sitting awkwardly in the sand to relieve his saddle sores. 'He wouldn't turn up to his own funeral without a flask on the hip.'

'But how does he afford it? I've been in town two years and I've never known him do a day's work.'

They were not really interested in the white-trash habits of Irish O'Neil. They were simply talking to help pass the long hours.

'He cadges mostly,' supplied Henri the Painter. 'But Friday and Saturday nights he makes the kid dance for pennies on the street, which he then splurges on red-eye quicker than you could spit.'

'Where I hail from we know how to deal with that breed,' Branson stated venomously. 'It's amazing how twenty strokes of the whip can improve a wastrel's conduct. Matter of fact, times like this makes one realize how sorely the whole town is in need of a clean-up. Drunks, neglected brats, gun hellions drifting in from Sonora interfering with our way of life . . .'

'Looks like Ethan is on his high horse again,' observed Dingus the blacksmith, leaning against an outcropping nearby. 'Could be his nose is out of joint on account Miss Jean seems to have took somethin' of a shine to Dulane.'

'Mebbe,' murmured Louis Dundee, raising his eyes to the hills. 'You reckon Buck and that Danny'll come back with the kid?'

'Well, I figure Buck's as good a trailsman as you'd find, while that Danny pilgrim. . . ? Well, there's somethin' about that young joker what makes you feel he don't make too many mistakes.'

131

'Yeah,' agreed the former lawman, running fingers through thinning hair. 'Guess he's something of a real odd one though, isn't he?'

'I didn't say that, did I, Louis?'

'Maybe not.'

The blacksmith was about to say more when the deep-throated roar of a shot came rolling down from Smoky Bluff.

Phil Reece peered through the saloon window to see Cheeko Rafer and the others toying with their drinks and making small-talk with the locals. It was near four in the morning with first light only an hour away but nobody felt like sleeping in Limbo. At least the outlaws were now fully informed on the cause behind all the nocturnal excitement. They could not care less about any runaway brat, or towners either absent or present for that matter. They had their job to do. Cheeko's was to take it easy at the Cobweb Palace and ensure his henchmen didn't overindulge. The gang boss estimated that they had had maybe twenty to twenty-four hours' lead on Trueno, in which time they could rest up plenty before taking their sweet time setting up an ambush that simply could not fail.

Even so, Rafer insisted that they should maintain at least one full-time look-out. Which was howcome Reece's feet ached from unaccustomed walking as he patrolled the town and kept a sharp eye out for any danger that might happen along while his brother hellions took their well-earned ease.

How was it he always drew the short straw, anyway?

It seemed an easy enough chore, he reflected, yet

knew he was very edgy. He had no trouble in coming up with the reason for that.

Trueno.

Down south, the gang had been made to look like hicks by Trueno so often that Reece and some of his henchmen had developed a kind of phobia about that bloody-handed *renegado* king of Diaz City.

Were it anyone but Trueno they were hunting, Phil Reece knew, he would be breathing easy and feeling good tonight. So he simply forced himself to relax about it all. As he turned away from the window a woman emerged from the batwings to stand on the porch facing north. He touched hatbrim and murmured 'Ma'am', but she did not seem to hear. She had some connection with the missing lad, he had overheard. Not a bad-looker, if she shucked that frumpy dress and used a little face-powder. But he figured she was dull, like the rest of this crummy town. 'See Limbo and die!' might well be a fitting slogan for this man's town. People kept reassuring him that the bunch had arrived right smack in the middle of the first bit of genuine excitement this place had seen in years, but excitement-starved Phil found this a little hard to believe. If they called sitting up all night waiting for a search-party to find some snotnose kid, imagine what it might do to the civic blood pressure if and when Trueno got to show up on these dusty streets!

Phil took his boredom for a walk around the perimeter, found it all quiet, just as expected.

Now at last he began genuinely to relax as he continued on his rounds, hands thrust behind his shell-belt, shoulders hunched high and hatbrim tugged low. He was humming tunelessly to himself as he sauntered by the dark recessed doorway of Chisum Mercantile where he didn't even think of pausing to take a closer look inside on the wild off-chance that it might possibly harbor the most dangerous Mexican *bandido* of them all packing four sixguns, a Bowie and a stiletto beneath his everyday brown jacket.

Had he done so, Diego Rivera would have had to silence him swiftly before he could raise the alarm for his trail-weary henchmen, who were at that very moment quitting the Cobweb Palace to catch forty winks at their back-street rooming-house.

Diego Rivera emerged to watch the receding figure in the moonlight. 'Phil Reece!' He whistled softly. 'Gun *segundo* to Cheeko Rafer. . . ! Trueno's hunch has proved out again. Our man's got to be someplace close, right enough!' The Mexican's nervous system thrummed with excitement as he stood massaging his neck and listening to the quiet.

He felt tempted to buttonhole some towner to ask after Rafer as well as a man known elsewhere as the Hanging Judge. Rivera actually considered this, but then rejected it. Sure, he could pass for a gringo – mostly. But if there was an alert out here for Mexican *bandidos* or anything at all that might connect them with either Trueno or Judge Ira Black, then he could easily tip their hand.

At this late stage of the leader's long hunt after Black, Rivera dared not risk this.

He decided instead to follow Phil Reece.

Big Phil led his tail all over this unusually insomniac town until eventually stopping by at an establishment called Mrs Torrance's Rooming-house on Harlan Street.

Rivera watched from the black moonshadow of a big old oak across the street until Reece emerged from the building chomping on a drumstick, his jacket-collar turned up against the early-morning chill.

When the man had gone, Rivera slunk across the roomer's courtyard to the stables, where a quick inspection revealed several big horses along with saddles, saddle bags, harness and rifles stacked against a wall. The quick flare of a match showed him the initials C.R. burned into the stock of a cumbersome Big Fifty rifle. Cheeko Rafer!

His face suddenly grim and tight, Rivera quit the tree-shaded yard and legged it for the bridge where his horse was stashed. He had all he needed to know.

CHAPTER 9

The one-eyed wrangler was boring her with his prattle but at least he'd succeeded in keeping her awake, no small feat considering that Miss Jean had barely slept in days. All knew she had lost a whole night's rest over the boy, but none knew of the strange restlessness that had been troubling her prior to that, a stirring of emotion and a secret unease about her feelings for a man she feared she might have come to love.

'Want to know the best advice on life I ever heard, Miss Jean?' enquired the gabby wrangler. 'Never play poker with a man named Slim. Never chow down at a place called Mom and Pop's. And never but never ever sleep with somebody whose troubles are worse than your own.'

He lowered his voice.

'And never weep for another woman's kid, you'll weep enough for your own someday.'

Whether this was genuine wisdom or whiskey-fuelled bunkum, Miss Jean did not know. Or care. She rose from her chair on the saloon porch and moved to the steps where she was surprised by a voice from the shadows.

'Any news on the boy, Miss Jean?'

'Madame!' she said in surprise as the woman appeared in tassled shawl with a scarf ornamented by moon and stars holding her hair. 'What are you doing abroad at this hour?'

The fortune-teller's eyes were in shadow. 'Waiting for news of my boy, of course.'

'Your boy? Surely you mean Johnny O'Neil?'

'I wait for my boy . . . and he always comes when I need him . . .'

Jean shivered. With nerves worn thin and exhaustion eating at her, she really was not ready for Madame Caspar's morbid weirdness tonight.

She made to speak but the older woman cut her off sharply. 'Go inside, young woman, and warn the others to stay out of sight. For I smelt the blood and just now I have seen Death stalking by on Harlan Street. But do not fret for the child as he is safe.' She turned and started off, shawl-draped arms widespread. 'Fear only for Limbo . . .'

The night muffled her words and madame was gone. Miss Jean stood listening and staring uncertainly along the breadth of the lamplit street in the direction of Harlan Street until the sudden murderous uproar of gunplay tore the night apart.

*

Only a true assassin of Rivera's skill was capable of stalking a pro like Reece. To reach Rafer's look-out Trueno's *segundo* was forced to snake his way flat on his belly for fifty yards across mostly open and moon-washed ground to reach his man undetected, where he paused soundlessly by the corral gate to light a cigar and check out his timepiece.

4:47.

By 4:48, eight inches of Spanish steel had driven into Reece's back and pierced his heart. 4:49 saw silent figures detach from the squat mass of the feed-store to make their way past the Harlan Street corrals and head for the rooming-house.

Trueno himself was leading them.

A gentle morning breeze rattled a blind-cord softly, and somewhere a trail-weary outlaw snored abruptly then was silent again. Shadows flitted by a moonwashed window and a sudden voice called: 'Who's that? That you, Phil?' The response was a gunblast that filled the dormitory room with a shimmering blue light, revealing hawk-faced figures in black Mexican *charro* fanning their guns' hammers swiftly and methodically to fill the room with death. With bodies pitching every which way and screams turning the night hideous about him, Cheeko Rafer alone escaped the death-room. The outlaw was a bull with a bull's brute power and animal determination. Triggering the pistol, Rafer blasted a dark figure from his path, then wrapped heavy arms protectively about his head and crashed headlong through a side-window like a torpedo.

He hit the porch floor in a spray of shattered glass, had sprung half-way to his feet when Trueno's lean gun-arm snaked through the jagged window and pumped three shots into him to hammer his blood-spurting body out into the flooding moonlight.

Rafer's face was exactly the same dust-gray as the earth beneath him as he lay on his back with legs and arms outspread, staring up at the lean and supple form propped against the sky. 'Trueno . . . you lousy stinking greaser son of a bitch! How. . . ?'

'A loser should always know his limitations, vermin.'

Caught between the double disappointment of dying a loser or fighting to stay alive for no purpose whatsoever, Rafer looked inwards to make a choice, unaware that Trueno's bullets had taken all choice out of his hands.

Seeing into the heart and soul of the dying killer, Trueno the timber-wolf saw the once fierce and deadly enemy now as timid and fearful as a little fox kit cornered by the hounds.

For Cheeko, it was so hard to let go and die this way, so hard to stay. It was hard all the way.

The heavy revolver churned one more time, the big body on the earth jumped once and it was over.

By this time his surviving men had emerged into the yard and Trueno belatedly realized, with a small sense of shock, just how costly it had proved to remove Cheeko Rafer. Sure, maybe now he was in a good position to get on with the task that had brought him a hundred miles from Musketoon Mountain, but at what price! All around the killer now, dazed-looking hotel guests were staring fearfully down from their bedroom windows and it seemed to them that they could still hear the stuttering echoes of the fierce minute of gunplay that had rocked Limbo from border to border.

Trueno calmly dumped the empty shell-casings from his revolver.

He felt less calm than he appeared.

He knew he must move swiftly before his real quarry had the chance to be alerted and escape!

'Find out where he is!' he snarled. Immediately one *bandido* clutching a bloodied arm and another with his right ear shot away obediently went to windows and doorways and straight away began barking the same urgent question.

Where was the man known as Branson, yet whose real name was Judge Ira Black?

Waiting wide-legged and heroic-looking in the middle of the street, Trueno calmly reloaded his revolver, paying no further attention to the staring carcass at his feet. Although Cheeko Rafer had been a threat, a rival and a thorn in his side for too long, arrogant Trueno had always dismissed the gunman as a nothing, hence there was but a limited sense of triumph to be found here. The true victory was yet to be taken.

Rivera came limping back to his leader.

'Black is here as we believed, *caudillo*,' he reported, grimacing in pain. 'Has been almost all the

140

two years.'

Suddenly Trueno felt the full jolt of the exhilaration which the the death of Rafer had failed to arouse in him.

'Ethan Branson . . . Judge Black. . . !' He rolled the names on his tongue. Then he snapped, 'Where does he live?'

'He . . . he is not here, Fidel. A child is missing and Black is out with the searchers.' Rivera jabbed a bony finger north. 'Out there . . .'

Trueno cursed viciously, then forced himself to focus. It was almost dawn. The sound of their gunshots would have travelled far; they had been sounds that might well alarm and alert a fearful and guilty man – such as the judge.

'How many with him and how far off are they?' he demanded to know.

Rivera glanced back at the terrified guests who'd supplied his information. 'Perhaps seven or eight in the party,' he reported. 'And they are searching somewhere between where we stand and those hills.' He winced, paused a moment, than added, '*Patron*, you must realize that only you, Miguel and myself are fit to ride. Perhaps we should wait until Black returns here rather than ride out—'

'I have waited two years.' Trueno cut him off, making an imperious gesture as he strode off. 'I shall not delay one moment longer. Come, *amigo*, and make sure you bring a rope.'

They could hear roosters crowing from some farm-yard far off to the east as they approached Twin

Rocks with dawn just touching the skies. Already the first birds were scampering in the bushes. The moon had finally lost its light and a scatter of high clouds was beginning to take color as they caught the first rays of a sun which the horsemen could not yet see. The wind blew coolly from the south and the weary horses picked up their shuffling gait as they caught the smell of the river.

Dulane glanced down at the small figure perched on the saddle-horn before him, then looked back. The towners were sitting straighter in their saddles now and appeared highly pleased with themselves in anticipation of the big welcome they reckoned they could expect when they rode back into the town. His eyes sought out Danny who, moments before, had been travelling at his side at the head of the column as the trail funnelled down into the pass between the rocks.

The youth was nowhere to be seen.

Before hipping around to look back, Dulane rubbed at his eyes and muttered a soft curse. As practical-minded as any man of his profession must be, he was deeply impressed by the slender youth who had been of such assistance during their hunt, but at the same time he was aware of something strange about him, something he could not quite identify, although it could well be his habit of 'vanishing' unexpectedly from time to time, then reappearing again.

'You must be tireder than you know, Dulane,' he muttered. Then he cursed when he realized that the strangely compelling youth was sitting very erect in his saddle opposite and staring seriously straight ahead.

'Where the hell. . . ?' he began tetchily, then broke off. What was he about to say that wouldn't sound foolish. He cleared his throat. 'What are you looking at, kid?' he grunted, his voice rising above the shuffle of hoofs in the dust.

'Nothing in particular. Just wondering about all that shooting we heard, is all . . .'

A celebration,' Dulane informed him tersely. 'Somehow the town must have heard that we found Johnny, so they just felt like whooping it up.'

Danny twisted in his saddle to stare back.

'I doubt Branson goes along with your notion. Look at him. He's been looking that way ever since we heard all that racket.'

Dulane looked. It was true that Branson appeared to be acting uncharacteristically, strangely; he was tense and fidgety. But Dulane just shrugged his shoulders and turned to the way ahead again. Nothing was going to distract or bother him this bright new morning. So he went right back to thinking thoughts such as he had never seriously thought before until coming to a town called Limbo. Crazy thoughts, so the back of his mind told him. Real foolish. But that did not stop him enjoying and encouraging them. And each time he thought of a woman with green eyes, he glanced at the kid travelling with them; he sensed that they must be good, honest and genuine thoughts even if they were likely plumb loco.

There was no warning.

As Dulane and Danny led the riders between twin giant cedars the Mexican horsemen simply erupted from cover with the strengthening daylight shimmering blue and menacing off naked gun barrels.

'*Alto*!' shouted the blocky one, and his rifle was trained squarely on Dulane's chest.

The searchers stopped in their tracks and Dulane felt a jolt of unreality. After the night they had been through the thought furthest from his mind had been more trouble. Had he been recklessly careless? If so, how could that be? What could armed and dangerous-looking Mexican *pistoleros* possibly have to do with events unfolding here? Who the blue hell were they?

Only one man seemed to know the answer to that, and Ethan Branson was fumbling for his belt gun as the tall and arrogant Mexican, obviously the leader, heeled his flashy mount forward, his face a cold mask of menace.

'Go ahead, Señor Black!' he said in a voice like iron. 'Bring out your gun if you dare. But it will not save you from justice and the hangrope!'

Branson froze and Dulane shook his head irritably in even deeper puzzlement.

'What the hell is this?' he demanded. 'Who are you geezers, anyway? What's this all about?'

'Not that it is any concern of yours, gringo,' replied the tall Mexican. 'But I am Trueno, and this excrement about to die is Ira Black, the hanging judge of Amarillo. Is that not the truth, "Señor Branson"?'

144

The judge was the color of death as his trembling hand slid slowly off his gun.

'This . . . this is monstrous!' he croaked. He hipped around in his saddle, looking desperately to his fellow citizens for support, for understanding as he explained. 'Gentlemen . . . friends, part of what this outlaw says is true. I once sat on the bench at Amarillo as a judge of the United States Court . . . and in one case it was my duty to sentence this butcher and his stinking brothers to death. But Trueno escaped and pledged to return and murder me for hanging his brothers. I . . . I had seen so much of him during the trial and learned so much of his murderous record in Sonora that I knew he was quite capable of carrying out his threat. And when Sonoran authorities took it upon themselves actually to warn me officially of my danger I was convinced that I had no option but to simply disappear. So I searched for the most innocent, obscure place I could find and I found Limbo.' His voice rose as he turned back to face the enemy. 'How did you find me, you murderous dog?'

'This man is all that was ever evil rolled into one,' Trueno counter-accused, the gun in his bronzed fist rock-steady. 'My brothers were little more than children and their crimes were not great, yet he placed them upon his accursed gibbet and snuffed out their sweet lives . . .'

Emotion choked off his voice. He signalled violently.

'Rivera, the rope. And you, Hanging Judge Black, step down and prepare to meet your Maker.'

145

Dulane stared around as the judge almost tumbled from his saddle. Foolishly, Black found himself searching for signs of support from the townsmen. All in vain. To a man they were frozen and cowed by this unforeseen danger, just as they had been earlier in the presence of *La Sombra.*

They were true cowards, Dulane realized with some anger. He knew in that instant that not only must he quit soulless Limbo when he was through here, but so too must others whom he cared for. That town was simply not good enough for them; it was, in the truest sense of the term, a noplace town for nobodies.

He at least half-way believed the accusations being levelled against the judge, was disgusted all the way down by the man's obvious terror as he faced his past. Yet knew he never could simply stand by and watch laws made by great men be broken.

He slid from his horse and stepped clear of it before anybody could stop him. Alone he faced the the ring of guns as Trueno's dark eyes glittered warningly. 'Did I tell any of you to move, *hombre?* Get rid of your weapons. Now! All of you!'

'Hold on to your weapons!' Dulane countered in a voice that rang with authority. He nodded at Trueno, bitter-eyed.

'You're not hanging this man,' he said stonily. He hadn't permitted an innocent child to perish and would not stand by and see any man murdered in cold blood. Even a Yankee soldier of fortune had his sense of justice. He did not see this as heroism, merely as what any man should do.

He didn't expect Trueno to react with such speed or fury. The Mexican's gun blurred upwards ready to fire, Boy Johnny screamed, Dulane was staring at sudden death – and then Danny was moving.

The youth heeled his horse between Dulane and Trueno. There was a roar of Colts and gunsmoke billowed thickly around the youth's slender figure. He appeared to sway in the saddle but did not fall in the moments that followed as a grim-jawed Dulane came clear with both guns with blistering speed. He had never shot faster or straighter; had never been in greater danger, nor had more vital reasons to live.

With gunsmoke roiling thickly and gun crashes thundering like the hammers of God, Buck Dulane provided a murderous exhibition of what he did best of all. Rivera staggered backwards with a sudden third eye in his forehead before he could pull trigger. Dulane dropped to one knee as Trueno leapt into sight from behind Danny's turning mount. The *bandido*'s face was black with fury, then white with fatal shock as Dulane's cannonade of .45 slugs stitched across his arching chest. Hurling himself violently sideways to roll in the dust ahead of spurting geysers of close bullet strikes, Dulane fanned gun hammer and a third man with his throat shot out pitched from his saddle, triggering into the sky as he went down.

It was shockingly quiet as Dulane lurched to his feet with blood soaking his thigh. He stood weaving and staring at the dead. Judge Black started weeping. Johnny jumped to the ground close to the still bodies, shivering. Nobody spoke. The surviving *bandidos* still outnumbered the citizens but their hands were now empty. These riders from Musketoon Mountain were cut from a very different cloth from Rivera and Trueno and appeared almost paralysed by the shock and suddenness of their leader's lightning-bolt death – by the whole crimson spectacle.

Everyone was staring at Dulane but he was watching Danny as the young man slid from his saddle and fingered his hat back from his brow.

Buck dashed at his eyes with the back of his hand. Something wrong with his eyes. This had happened before when that boy was around. Sometimes when he looked at Danny the young man appeared somehow fuzzy around the edges, insubstantial somehow.

It was almost eerie, inexplicable.

But there could be no denying that the young man had surely saved his life by blocking Trueno's line of fire for those vital moments. Yet the astonishing thing was that, although he was certain he'd seen Trueno give both barrels to the young man at close range, Danny appeared to show no sign of injury. Slowly he shook his head. Didn't make sense.

He realized that there was no time to dwell on incidentals as he limped across to lift Boy Johnny to his shoulder. He stood staring bleakly around at the killing ground as though half expecting that the next disaster would jump up out of the ground as . . . as killer lions and badmen from Sonora had already done tonight.

But realized slowly that it really was over.

By chance and circumstance, Limbo had been

violently jolted from its drowsy years of anonymity and isolation by terror and danger, but already the dust was plainly beginning to settle again.

The sun came over the rim as it did every morning and a new day was on the march.

Looked like being a hot one.

CHAPTER 10

THREE NORTH

'But why would he simply disappear?' wondered Jean Kelly as they watched Dulane light up his after-lunch cigarette. 'He's the town hero ... well, I mean, you both are, of course. Are you sure he wasn't hurt in the shooting, Buck? Everyone seemed certain he had been hit. Perhaps he's gone off to heal himself, or—'

'He wasn't hurt.' Dulane was emphatic. 'And he was fine last anyone saw of him. Far as I can tell that would have been Doc. Told me he saw Danny down by Madame Caspar's, riding along the river.' He grinned uneasily. 'Matter of fact Doc said he saw him one moment in clear sight by the bridge but next time he looked he was just gone.'

He studied the woman intently as he spoke but she offered no sign of response. He assumed she had no reason to believe there might be something strangely unusual about madame's son. The same applied to the men in the street, some of whom even appeared puzzled or uncomprehending whenever Dulane mentioned the youth now, like they weren't quite sure who in hell he was talking about.

Strange? Surely. Yet not half as strange or improbable as the grim fact that not one but two bands of bloody-handed badmen had descended upon drowsy, dreamy Limbo in the past week and that menace and danger had somehow been dealt with and cast aside in a manner any 'normal' American town would have to be proud of.

A silence descended at the front-window table of the diner where the day's special was still NO CREDIT.

He torched a stogie into life and his thoughts refused to leave the slender young man who'd made such a vivid impression upon himself, Boy Johnny and Jean Kelly. He shrugged. The youth had appeared seemingly from nowhere and it seemed almost fitting that he should leave the same way.

'I'm going to miss Danny,' Boy Johnny said somberly. Then, childlike, he slid from his chair with an eager grin. 'There's my friend Oscar. Hey, Oscar, I'll tell you about the lion.'

The couple watched him run out onto the eatery porch, then turned to each other, not speaking but with expressions every bit as eloquent as a booming Baptist preacherman up in his pulpit persuading his flock to renounce the occasions of mortal sin.

It was all too plain to both now something quite astonishing had happened to them in the wake of the bloodbath, something that seemed to have greatly accelerated what at first had been simply an easy friendship between a man and a woman, subtly shaping it into something infinitely more.

Jean intended leaving Limbo and Buck Dulane knew he must also eventually go. Was there any valid reason why they shouldn't travel together ? This was the totally unexpected thought which had first lodged in Dulane's brain directly in the wake of that final murderous shootout. He had thought of little else all day as he watched shell-shocked citizens going about the necessary business of picking up the pieces of a town that had almost, but not quite, seen itself blown off the county map.

At last he began to speak.

He had a plan, he told her. Nothing monumental or earth-shattering, but a plan nontheless. Jean had already sold up and had indicated her intention of visiting Nevada, where gold was booming and opportunities seemed to abound. Dulane thought Nevada might suit him also – that was if she might appreciate a little company? He suggested they might travel together – just for company, he made clear. But she had been through a lot and and he genuinely didn't believe she should be alone. He supposed that applied to them all – her, himself, Boy Johnny.

What did she think?

'I . . . I think it sounds wonderful, Buck. But . . but what about your . . . should I call it a profession. . . ?'

'I've finished with the guns.'

It was the simplest yet most momentous of statements. But true. He knew it to be so and somehow his total conviction seemed to convince her that she could believe it also.

She reached across the table and squeezed his hand. She thought it sounded wonderful, she said, and very practical and sensible as well. But she must be truthful. Now that the time had come for her to leave Limbo and move on, she somehow felt anchored here as never before.

'You mean . . . by the kid?' he guessed.

'I'm afraid so. You see, Buck, I know now that that child has meant more to me all along than I would permit myself to admit. I feared allowing him to grow too close. But . . . but after all the dangers he survived, I think I realized . . .' She paused. 'Why are you holding your finger to your lips, Buck?'

'Just want to ask you a question. Would you still go north with me if the boy could go with us?'

'Why, of course, but how. . . ? I mean, his uncle . . .'

'Maybe I can do a deal with Irish.' He rose quickly and dropped money on the table. 'I'll go see him, Jean . . . it's at least worth a try.'

He had at least a hundred solid reasons for feeling good as he limped his way along the street, but there were just as many negatives when a man paused and looked about him. Limbo was still reeling in the aftermath of the greatest upheaval in its placid back-water history. When the hanging judge had selected this remote town by the big river as the perfect hide-away he had unwittingly targeted it for a disaster two years in the coming. But with 'Branson' finally exposed and Miss Jean fixing to leave, and the entire community struggling to get back on its feet again, it appeared that the going would be tough here for quite a spell.

And yet he sensed it would survive well enough and perhaps even one day grow strong and shake off the stifling grip of the past, in time.

Sure it could survive, with luck. As might Buck Dulane, Jean Kelly and little Boy Johnny – also with luck, and maybe a little extra something on the side.

He found Irish at the saloon knocking back cold ones and reliving 'an uncle's anguish', suffered during the drama involving his nephew.

The man jumped a foot when Dulane approached behind a big grin. He didn't trust Buck one inch, was still aching all over from their last encounter. But Buck Dulane could turn on the charm like a tap when it suited. He also bought his man a full bottle of prime sourmash for himself right then and there to help 'ease the pain' of his recent ordeal, before cordially inviting him to join him for a private discussion on the child's immediate future. Irish O'Neil was so taken in that by the time they reached the old shed in the saloon yard he was unburdening himself on how he really felt about the human burden he'd been saddled with by fate.

'Nobody knows what I go through with that kid, Dulane. This getting lost caper of his is just the latest heartache he's caused me and I don't mind telling you that—'

'How would you like him out of your hair? I mean, permanent?'

'Huh?' Irish's wet lips hung open. His eyes were suspicious. Dulane's question didn't seem to hit right. 'How do you mean, er, Buck?'

'I agree the boy must be one hell of a burden, Irish. A solid, respectable fellow like you expected to nursemaid a grubby little brat who doesn't give a shucks for anybody? How rough is that? Well, the truth is that Miss Kelly and I have made plans to move on north right now, and it was her idea that maybe we should do you a Christian charity kindness and make an offer to take the kid off your hands. You know, take him with us, look after him, give you a break and—'

'How dare you!'

'Huh?'

Irish O'Neil could fake outrage better than any Poet's Corner actor. 'You'd take my meal-ticket, er, I mean . . . my flesh and blood, my late brother's only boy—?'

'Not for nothing,' Dulane cut in, removing his hat. He rubbed forefinger and thumb together in the universal signal for money. 'Hell's bells, man, you don't think we'd expect you to give up, as you say, your own flesh and blood without compensation!'

'Compensation?' Irish's eyes rolled in red-rimmed sockets. 'You are talking money?'

'Real money. More money most likely than you've had at one time in your unlucky life. What do you say?'

Irish O'Neil didn't even bother feigning outrage any longer. Avarice had him by the throat and appeared to be choking him. 'How much?'

Dulane turned his hat upside down. Stitched into the crown was an oilskin envelope from which he slid a slim leather billfold, which he opened with a flick of his finger to reveal a wad of large denomination banknotes. By this time the barfly was visibly salivating.

'Five hundred.' Buck grinned, counting big bills into an eager palm. He closed Irish's fingers tightly over the notes, his smile maybe a little wolfish now. 'Five hundred more than you've ever had in your life, in return for which you agree to let the kid go with us and promise you'll never bother him or lay any claim to him again. Right?'

Irish was almost weeping in wonderment. But even as he pumped Dulane's hands and gave his solemn promises there was the latent glitter of avarice and cunning in his red-rimmed eye which Dulane could read only too plainly.

'Of course, by the time you've blown all this on the booze, you'll come up with the bright notion that you could track us down and squeeze me some more,' he said. 'Which I guess would be understandable enough – if only you were less of a total son of a bitch.'

Irish stared. 'Huh?'

Dulane was not smiling any longer.

'I've seen the scars on that lad,' he said icily. 'Ones that you put there. Real scars. A man shouldn't get away with that, Irish . . . kid like that should never be bothered again by the likes of you as long as he lives, and won't be. Just remember that – and this.'

The blow to the head knocked the drunk clear off his feet. He rolled and moaned, then began to bleat until a boot drove into his squishy guts, cutting off his breath. In the handful of seconds that followed, Irish O'Neil absorbed more brutal punishment than he'd done over a full boozehound's lifetime.

Eventually he was hauled to his feet, a bloodied, trembling wreck. He dazedly found Buck Dulane's grim face a bare inch from his own.

'If you ever come within fifty miles of us – *ever*, I'll finish what I just started here just now, scum. Savvy?'

Irish could barely speak. 'S . . . savvy, Buck. Savvy!'

Dulane let him drop like a bag of trash and stepped out into the bright day. He was smiling. Sometimes it made a man feel real good to act real mean.

The whole town turned out in the twilight to watch the rubber-tired buggy carry them out along Boot Hill Road which eventually joined up with the Northwest Trail – Dulane, Jean Kelly and the child.

The mayor gave a cheer and it was taken up by a hundred voices that faded slowly as the rig rolled by the undertaker's, the feed-and-grain barn and McCloskey's ramshackle shotgun cabin, the last building in the row.

Plying the reins, Dulane shot a sideways glance at the woman and the boy, Jean thoughtful and grave, Boy Johnny leaning forward eagerly with a half-eaten apple someone had given him in his hand.

The past was already drifting away behind and the future beckoned uncertainly ahead.

No concrete plans had been made, yet all three sensed – even the child – that whatever was waiting up north for them would be good. They could feel it, and the feeling was exhilarating.

Dulane's leg ached some yet he was feeling drowsy and comfortable enough while Miss Jean drove. Boy Johnny's eager gaze swept over the mysterious, slowly darkening landscape as the rooftops of town sunk in back of them and they rolled past the TO BOOT HILL sign without a second glance. The adults barely noticed at first when Johnny yawned sleepily and said casually; 'There's Danny.'

Dulane grunted and stirred, then settled back again. But a small hand tugged at his shirt. 'Buck, it's Danny!'

Jean brought the rig to a sharp halt in the middle of the trail as Dulane hauled himself erect. They stared back at the boy then peered ahead into the deepening dusk. At first all they saw was nothing but a strip of receding white road which eventually dipped from sight into a grassy hollow where a gently swaying cypress and a white-painted sign bearing the single word 'Cemetery' were dimly visible above overgrown trailside grasses.

Then they saw him . . . or did they? It was hard to be sure in this fast-fading light.

Certainly there was something up ahead on the road, a misty yet curiously substantial-seeming figure on horseback riding in the same direction as themselves and approaching the dip in the trail a hundred yards ahead. It seemed the slender young man astride a familiar white horse had materialized from the dusk.

Dulane rubbed at his eyes and for some reason felt a chill pass over him, shaking his entire body. He cleared his throat and called, 'Danny? That you?'

No response.

At first the rider did not seem to hear as he began receding down the slope until only his upper body was visible above the rim, where a broken picket-fence encircled an area studded by wooden markers standing crookedly in uncut grass. The riders in the rig caught their breath when the dimming figure turned his head slightly and raised a goodbye hand before lifting his face to the darkening sky – and was gone.

The buggy horse pulled up of its own accord as three pale faces stared ahead in total silence.

Had they seen what they thought they had – the momentarily clear-cut silhouette of Danny Caspar, the raising of a goodbye hand and then that dimly shimmering light.

They climbed down, Jean staring up at Buck wonderingly. But he was staring at the ground at his feet. There were no hoofprints where man and horse had been.

He cleared his dry throat and each took the boy by the hand and went uncertainly forward to bring the silent cemetery into full view, with the rickety old fence encircling it and the small grave which caught the eye as it alone was marked by a jar filled with freshly cut wildflowers.

Evening fog wisped silently between old tomb-stones as those last rays of twilight appeared to illuminate the headstone like a ghostly beam. Uneasy, curious, they moved on down to the graveside to study the hand-cut inscription, which read:

DANIEL JAMES CASPAR
DROWNED LIMBO 1871
R.I.P.
AGED THREE AND A HALF YEARS

HE SLEEPS WITH JESUS

Dulane and Jean stared at one another in wonder, the boy looking up at them. Nobody spoke. There was something strange and powerful in the very air that touched and held each one, which each could feel but could not identify. Yet intuitively all three seemed to be strangely invested with a great wisdom which enabled them to half-understand things they might never speak of, yet which they sensed, even then, might somehow bring comfort and reassurance in the years ahead.

Hand in hand they returned to the rig and drove on slowly, gazing back to see the evening wind gently brushing the long grass where a child named Danny slept.